Liam let the camera lens move along the length of her body

From his surveillance point, he had a clear view of her through her bedroom window. He watched as she pulled her T-shirt over her head. Her jeans were next and she skimmed them off her hips and kicked them away. "Hmm, black underwear. Pretty racy for an accountant," he murmured to himself.

He'd been given a picture of her when he'd accepted the job, but that woman had been all conservative and efficient looking, nothing like this beautiful, sensual lady. But Eleanor Thorpe was a suspect in the embezzlement of a quarter million dollars. What better way to pull off a crime than to play the dependable, quietly forgettable employee?

But now she was reaching around for the hook on her bra and Liam's mouth went dry.

He was about to get an insider's look at just how *unforgettable* Eleanor Thorpe could be....

Dear Reader,

The Quinns are back! For those of you who read my first
MIGHTY QUINNS trilogy, I'm sure you probably realized
that I couldn't just leave the younger brothers—Brian,
Sean and Liam—living life as carefree bachelors. After
all, what fun would that be?

The Quinn family has always done its best to avoid
commitment. But the three youngest brothers have
more to deal with than just the old family legends—
where all the men are heroes and the women are
schemers. Now there's a new Mighty Quinn "curse."
After brothers Conor, Dylan and Brendan each rode to
the rescue of a beautiful woman in distress, they ended
up tumbling helplessly into love. Can Brian, Sean and
Liam avoid the same fate? Or will destiny give them
their own chance at happily-ever-after?

I hope you enjoy Liam's story. And watch for Brian and
Sean coming in the following months. And then who
knows? There are probably a few Quinn cousins out
there waiting to find romance.

Happy reading,

Kate Hoffmann

P.S. I love to hear from my readers. Visit my Web site at
www.katehoffmann.com for news about all my books,
past, present and future.

Books by Kate Hoffmann

THE MIGHTY QUINNS miniseries

Harlequin Single Title—REUNITED

Kate Hoffmann
THE MIGHTY QUINNS: LIAM

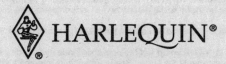

HARLEQUIN®

TORONTO • NEW YORK • LONDON
AMSTERDAM • PARIS • SYDNEY • HAMBURG
STOCKHOLM • ATHENS • TOKYO • MILAN • MADRID
PRAGUE • WARSAW • BUDAPEST • AUCKLAND

For my great-great-great-great-grandfather Patrick Doolin,
who provided me with my only drop of Irish blood.

ISBN 0-373-69133-5

THE MIGHTY QUINNS: LIAM

Copyright © 2003 by Peggy A. Hoffmann.

This edition published by arrangement with Harlequin Books S.A.

Visit us at www.eHarlequin.com

Printed in U.S.A.

___Prologue___

THE THREE BOYS hunched down on the floor of the front parlor, peering through the tattered lace curtains at a figure on the front porch.

"What should we do?" Liam Quinn whispered. "We can't let her in."

"Answer the door," his brother Brian ordered. "We have to pretend everything is okay."

"She'll go away," Sean reassured them both. "Just wait." Sean was Brian's twin and they usually disagreed on everything.

"No," Liam whispered. "She's not going away. Not this time."

A knot of fear twisted in his stomach and he held his breath. He and his five brothers had been dodging social workers long enough for Liam to know exactly what they looked like. This one wore a gray coat, nearly the same color as the dirty snow that melted on either side of the street. But it was the dour expression and overstuffed briefcase that really gave her away.

"Answer the damn door," Brian snapped. "Just tell her you're home sick and Da is napping in the bedroom."

Liam turned to his older brothers, the twins both glaring at him. He was the swing vote, a position very difficult for a ten-year-old. "What if she wants to talk to him, Einstein?"

"You'll just have to convince her that he can't be bothered," Brian explained. "Tell her he has a contagious flu...and that he's barfing...and that the doctors said he has to sleep. You can do it, Li." Brian gave him an encouraging pat on the shoulder.

The doorbell buzzed again and Liam jumped at the harsh sound. The social workers had been a fear for as long as he could remember. They were like the mythical dragons in their father's tales of the Mighty Quinn ancestors, always lurking in the shadows and waiting to swoop down to tear their family to shreds.

Winter was the worst season for the dragons to strike. In the winter, there was no way they could produce a responsible parent. In late October, Seamus Quinn took *The Mighty Quinn* down to the Caribbean, following the swordfishing fleet to warmer waters where he'd earn a winter income not possible on the North Atlantic. Since he was due to return at the beginning of April, they were still on their own for a few more weeks.

Liam didn't exactly have a perfect family, but it was as close as the six Quinn brothers would ever come. Though his older brothers remembered a time when things were better, Liam had never known any other life. Conor, Dylan, Brendan and the twins, Sean and Brian, had all been born in Ireland, a country Liam only knew as an island on a map. But to hear them speak of it, Ireland had been a land filled with magic and mystery and wonderful, happy times.

Liam had tried to imagine what it was like to have a

regular family, a father who came home every night and a mother who cooked dinner and read stories. But all that was over by the time Liam joined the family. Their father, Seamus, had brought his wife and five sons to America before Liam was even born. He'd bought a partnership in Uncle Padriac's long-liner, *The Mighty Quinn*, working at an occupation that took him away from South Boston for weeks and sometimes months at a time.

Liam had been the first Quinn born in America. He had always harbored a secret guilt that maybe he'd been the cause of his family's problems. He'd pieced together enough bits of information from whispered conversations between his brothers to know that everything had gone bad about the time he was born. His father had begun drinking and gambling, his mother often shut herself in her room and wept, and when they were together, they fought all the time.

And then she was gone. Conor had been eight at the time, old enough to remember her. Dylan had been six and remembered even less, and, at five, Brendan had only vague memories. As for the three-year-old twins and infant Liam, they'd been left to only imagine the dark-haired beauty who'd sung them lullabies and tucked them into bed.

"Fiona," Liam murmured, his lips forming her name like a charm against evil. If she were here, he wouldn't be scared. She was a Quinn, too, and she'd be strong enough to slay the dragon waiting on the porch. "The dragon is leaving."

The social worker turned and started down the front steps, but suddenly she returned to the door, this time pounding on the weathered wood with her fist. "I know you're in there," she shouted. "Mr. Quinn, if you don't let me in, I'm going to have to involve the police. Your three youngest sons didn't show up at school today. They're truant again."

Why they had to interfere, Liam didn't understand. He and his brothers were doing just fine. Conor was seventeen now and he had a part-time job that helped pay the bills. And Dylan and Brendan watched over things at home while their father was gone, picking up odd jobs when they could to add to the family treasury. And the twins, Sean and Brian, did chores around the house.

They managed pretty well as long as they stayed out of trouble. He cursed inwardly. Maybe skipping school that day hadn't been the smartest move, but sometimes the twins could be so persuasive. Besides, they rarely invited him along on their adventures, so he'd been flattered by the invitation.

Liam turned his attention back to the porch. He knew the real reason why they'd asked him today. He served as a good excuse. If they got caught by Conor, Sean and Brian would convince Liam to lie about how he'd had a stomachache or a headache and his twin brothers had been generous enough to stay home with him.

"She'll call the cops," Sean muttered. "They'll bust down the door and take us all away."

"All right, I'll do it," Liam said. "But you'll owe me."

"Anything," Sean said.

"My choice of your baseball cards—and yours," he

said, turning to Brian. "Any ten I want. No dibs or saves."

"No way!" Brian protested.

"Give him what he wants," Sean insisted. "He'll get rid of her. She'll believe him. People always like Liam."

Though it was a backhanded compliment, Liam relished it anyway. People did seem to trust him and he did have a knack for disarming most adults. Wasn't that why the twins always took him along when they planned to pinch candy from the corner store? If they got caught, Liam could always charm the store owner into letting them off the hook.

"Six cards," Brian said. "Three from each of us."

"Any ten that I want," Liam said. "And you have to help me study for all my math tests and my spelling tests for a month. And you have to do whatever I say for the rest of the day." He knew he was pushing it, but Liam so rarely had any power in the Quinn household.

"No way," Brian said.

"Deal," Sean countered.

Brian gave his twin a shove. "Who made you the boss?" A moment later he was pinned on the dusty parlor rug, Sean's knee pressed into the small of his back. "All right, all right. Deal."

"You guys go into Da's room," Liam said. "Close the curtains and crawl under the covers and pretend you're him. I might have to prove he's here. And don't make any snoring noises. Make it look good."

"Just get her out of here before Conor and Dylan

and Brendan get home. They'll kill us if they know we let her in."

"You just do your job," Liam said, walking to the door. "And I'll do mine."

When the twins got to the back of the house, Liam waited a few seconds then pulled the door open a crack. He tried to appear frightened. "What to you want? I'm gonna call the cops if you don't go away."

The lady stared down at him with a stern expression. "I'm Mrs. Witchell from County Social Services. I'd like to see your father, Mr. Seamus Quinn."

"He's sleeping," Liam said. "And he said I'm not supposed to let any strangers in."

"What are you doing home from school?"

"I'm sick. I have a fever."

"You can let me in," she said, showing him her identification. "I'm not going to hurt you. I'm just here to help."

Liam shut the door, then grabbed his coat from the pile near the radiator. He slipped out the door, closing it firmly behind him. "I'm not supposed to let anyone inside. But I guess I can talk to you out here." He sat on the top step, then patted the spot beside him. Mrs. Witchell smiled weakly at his invitation before she sat. "Why do you want to talk to my da?"

"Some of the neighbors are concerned. They say you boys are here on your own. That they haven't seen your father since before Thanksgiving."

"No," Liam said. "My dad is here. He has a job where he works at night so he sleeps during the day."

"That's not what they tell me," she said. "They say he's off fishing."

He shrugged. "Then they don't know what they're talking about."

"I really need to talk to your dad."

Liam tried to summon some tears, and when one dribbled down his cheek, he said, "He'll be mad at me if I let you in. And if you wake him up, he'll be madder still. Can't he just call you on the phone? I'll tell him to call as soon as he wakes up."

"I'm afraid that won't be good enough."

Liam paused. He had to play this very carefully. He had a sense that Mrs. Witchell wasn't easily charmed. But he could also tell that her determination was wavering. "Would you like a cup of coffee? I suppose you could wait inside until he wakes up. Then I wouldn't be in trouble."

"That would be all right," she said.

Liam stood. It was a risky move, letting her in the house. But he had to make her believe that he wasn't hiding anything. He held the door open for her and she nodded, clearly impressed with his manners. When they got inside, Liam helped her off with her coat, then showed her into the front parlor. Luckily, Conor and Dylan had cleaned the house last night. Though the furniture was tattered and stained, the room looked tidy.

"I'll just get you coffee," Liam said. He hurried to the back of the house and put the teakettle on, then tiptoed to his father's room. In the darkness he could make out a huge lump beneath the bedcovers. "Stay in bed," he whispered. "She's in the house."

Brian bolted upright. "You let her in? Jaysus, I knew we couldn't trust you to do this. What's she doing?"

"I'm making her coffee," Liam said.

"Aw, hell."

"Just pretend you're Da. I'll get her out as fast as I can." Liam softly shut the door behind him, then turned to find Mrs. Witchell watching him from the end of the hallway. Liam cleared his throat. "He's not awake yet. I'll just get your coffee."

She followed him into the kitchen and Liam watched as she carefully examined the room. Like the parlor, the kitchen was a bit shabby but still neat. "Who does the cooking?"

"Oh, my da," Liam said, dumping a good measure of instant coffee into a clean mug. "He loves to cook. And he's a good cook, too."

"What about when he's out on the boat?"

"Then Mrs. Smalley takes care of us. She's a good cook, too." Liam said a silent prayer that the social worker wouldn't insist on a conversation with Mrs. Smalley. Though Seamus paid her a small salary to serve as their baby-sitter, she usually didn't show up. And when she did, she was always drunk. Conor had told her long ago that they didn't need her help, even though Seamus continued to pay her.

The teakettle screeched and Liam snatched it up from the stove. He'd watched Conor make coffee a hundred times, his brother's choice of drink when he had to stay up late to study. He grabbed the sugar bowl and scooped a generous measure into the bottom of the cup before filling it with hot water. "Do you want milk?" he asked.

A smile broke across Mrs. Witchell's face as he handed her the cup. "No, this is fine." She took a sip and then winced. "It's very good." For a long moment she stared at him, then sighed. "I really have to be going. I have another appointment in a half hour. I'm just going to go talk to your father."

"But he's not awake," Liam pleaded.

She stared down at him for a long moment, then sighed. "All right, why don't I just look in on your father, just to make sure he's here with you? Then I'll leave my card and you can have him call me once he wakes up."

Liam gave her a wide smile, the kind of smile that all the girls at school seemed to like. "All right," he said. "But you have to promise to be quiet."

She set her cup down and Liam grabbed her hand, pulling her along to the bedroom. He pushed open the door and allowed her to step inside. The lump on the bed breathed roughly, a perfect mimic by the twins. Liam quickly pulled the social worker back out of the room and shut the door.

"Fine," she murmured.

By the time Liam showed her out, he could barely contain his relief. He watched her descend the front steps and walk down the block to her car, and as it drove by, he let out a loud whoop. A few seconds later Sean and Brian emerged from the bedroom. "She's gone!"

Sean grabbed Liam around the waist and gave him a fierce hug. "I knew you could do it. What did she say?"

Liam handed him the card. "She said Da is supposed to call her. Today." He turned to Brian. "Go get your cards. I want my ten."

The twins looked at each other, Brian balking at the request. "We made a deal," Sean admitted.

Liam settled onto the sofa and after Brian and Sean presented him with their treasured collections, he silently flipped through them, weighing the value of the cards he wanted. "Go get me some chocolate milk," he ordered Sean. "And you have to tell me a story," he said to Brian.

"No way," Brian cried.

"You promised. If you don't tell me a Mighty Quinn story, then I get twenty cards instead of ten."

"Tell him a story," Sean ordered.

"You tell him," Brian countered.

"I'm getting him chocolate milk. And you're better at stories."

"Tell me the one about the boy with the silver tongue," Liam said. "I like that one."

"This is the story of Riagan Quinn," Brian began. "Riagan was a foundling—"

"His father was killed in battle," Liam interjected.

"And his dying mother left him in the forest," Brian continued grudgingly. "And no one knew his real name, or where he came from. The fairies gave him the name Riagan 'cause it meant 'little king.' The forest was wild with wolves, but the fairies watched over him, feeding him drops of dew from their wands."

"Magic drops of dew," Liam added.

"Yeah, but that comes later. I'm not supposed to tell that part first."

Liam snuggled down on the sofa, distractedly examining a Bucky Dent card as his brother's voice wove the familiar tale. He loved the Mighty Quinn stories, especially this one. When his father or one of his older brothers decided to tell a story, Liam could almost picture Ireland. Brendan was the best storyteller and then his da. But in his da's stories, the women were always the enemy and Liam wasn't sure he liked that.

"One day, a poor beggar woman wandered into the forest, looking for food for her starving family and she came upon the wee child. But where were the babe's parents? she wondered. They were probably doing the same thing she was, gathering food in the forest. So she sat and waited for them to return."

"But they never came because Riagan didn't have parents," Liam said.

"He did. No one knew who they were," Brian said.

"No, he didn't. He was an orphan," Liam said.

"If you know the story so good, then why don't you tell it?" Brian snatched the Bucky Dent card away. "You can't have that one. Take the Carlton Fisk."

"As darkness fell, the woman began to worry," Liam said, prompting him to continue as he clamped his fingers on the Bucky Dent card and pulled.

Brian gave up the card. "She couldn't leave the baby in the woods for surely he'd be eaten by the wolves. But she already had seven children to feed at home. She walked away, but her heart had been captured by Riagan's sweet smile. In the end, she returned and carried him out of the woods. The fairies watched from the shadows, happy to see that Riagan had found a loving home."

Just then, the front door opened and Conor stepped inside. He shrugged out of his jacket, then glanced over at his brothers, giving them a suspicious look.

"What are you three up to? You're supposed to be doing your homework when I come home."

"A story," Liam said. "A Mighty Quinn story. Come and tell it. Brian doesn't do it the right way. It's the one about Riagan and the silver tongue." Conor groaned, but he didn't refuse. In truth, Conor rarely refused Liam anything. "The lady found him in the forest and took him home. That's where we are," Liam prompted.

Conor sat between Brian and Liam, throwing his arms along the back of the sofa. He tipped his head back and closed his eyes, then began to spin the tales that had become a regular part of their evenings together. There were so many Mighty Quinn tales to choose from, all of them featuring one of their long-ago ancestors, all of them exciting and heroic.

"Riagan settled into his new family," Conor said. "And soon their fortunes seemed to change. Everyone in the village came to see the baby and were so captivated by him that they left small gifts of food and clothing. And as Riagan grew, he became more and more handsome. And the drops of dew that the fairies had fed him had given him a silver tongue. Riagan could talk anyone into anything."

Liam snuggled against his brother's side, his earlier fears fading. Everything would be all right. Conor would make it right.

"Around the time Riagan was growing tall and strong, the king died and Queen Comyna came into power over the people of Ireland. She was greedy and suspicious and coveted all things of beauty and value, believing these things to be reserved for those of noble birth. And while her husband was generous with the poor people of his kingdom, his queen wasn't. She went through the kingdom, stripping her subjects of even the tiniest valuables. Times were hard and many people went hungry."

"But Riagan was a clever boy," Liam continued.

"Yes, he was. One day, while he was fishing in a stream, he came across a shallow pool, the bottom lined with pretty pink stones worn smooth by running water. He gathered them up and when he got back to his village, he sought out one woman in town, a woman known as a gossip. Riagan showed her one of the stones and told her that a fairy had given it to him and that it was more valuable than gold."

At that moment Dylan and Brendan came bursting through the front door, joking and laughing. They caught sight of their four brothers lined up on the sofa. "What's this?" Dylan asked.

"A story," Liam said. He motioned them over. "Brendan, you tell now."

Of all the Quinn brothers, Brendan had a special way with words, and if Liam closed his eyes and listened to Bren, he could see the story as if it were a movie in his head.

Conor continued, giving Brendan his cue. "Of course, the story about the pink stone spread quickly around the kingdom and, a few days later, Queen Comyna's soldiers showed up at Riagan's door, demanding that he turn over the fairy stones he'd found. But Riagan told them that the fairy had only given him one."

Brendan sat on the floor and stretched his legs out in

front of him. "The next day Riagan retrieved another pink stone from his hiding place and took it to town, telling the gossip that the fairy had visited him again. This time, a local merchant paid him a tidy sum for the fairy stone, but, as expected, the queen's soldiers soon came to collect the stone from the merchant. Time passed, and again and again, Riagan brought the fairy stones to town. And each time, the wealthy merchants fought to buy them from Riagan, certain that if the queen was collecting the stones, they must be of great value."

"I love this story," Liam murmured.

Bren smiled. "Finally, the day came when the queen's soldiers came to Riagan's house again and took him away to the palace. Queen Comyna demanded that Riagan give her all the stones he possessed, but Riagan told her that the fairy only gave him one stone at a time, for these stones were very powerful. Once a person possessed them all, they would be granted anything they wished for—wealth, beauty, youth, happiness."

Liam wondered where he might be able to find a stream in Boston. All he and his brothers needed were a few pink stones. They could use them to keep the family safe. And they could use them for food and to pay the heating bill.

"Now, no one knew how Riagan was able to convince the queen of this fantastic tale, but, many years later, they said it was his silver tongue, which he'd gotten from drinking the dewdrops from the tips of the fairies' wands. But many believed that Riagan was just a very clever boy, for he not only convinced the queen that the pink stones were more precious than diamonds or gold, he convinced her that trading all her possessions for the remainder of the stones could only increase her wealth a hundredfold. For all those possessions could be immediately replaced simply by wishing for them and so much more."

"So the greedy queen offered him everything," Liam said.

"Riagan walked home to retrieve the rest of the stones and, on they way, had to walk through the deep woods where he'd been found as a baby. There he met a fairy who appeared before him in a beam of light."

"Riagan, you have returned," Dylan interrupted in a high, squeaky voice. "You have shown yourself to be a kind and clever lad, but now you must become a man and take your rightful place as king. Give the stones to Comyna and she will offer all she owns. Take it. It is your birthright, but you must rule as King Ailfrid did, with compassion and a generous spirit."

This was the part in which their father usually launched into a long lecture about trusting women, about how all women were greedy and deceitful at heart, and how Ailfrid met his ruin because he loved Comyna and was blinded to her evil side. But Conor and Brendan usually left those parts out.

"And so the charming boy learned of his charmed life," Brendan said. "Riagan took his place on the throne, and during his reign, the kingdom flourished. And in a crofter's cottage at the edge of the dark forest, the greedy Comyna lived out her days, with only a bagful of pink stones found on the bottom of a small stream, knowing she had been bested by the boy with the silver tongue."

Brendan reached over and ruffled Liam's hair. "How was that?"

"Good," Liam murmured with a smile. "I feel better now."

Conor frowned. "What was wrong before?"

Liam heard Sean suck in a sharp breath and Brian nudged him in the ribs, a silent plea to keep his mouth shut. But Liam knew better. Conor was the only one who could keep them all safe. He was the Mighty Quinn and he'd find a way to keep the dragons from descending on the house.

"We skipped school today," Liam said. "And a social worker came to visit."

1

LIAM QUINN'S NOSE itched as he stepped into the musty attic, dust kicking up with every step. The place smelled of old wood and the floorboards creaked beneath his feet. A decrepit horsehair couch sat in the corner, and against the far wall he saw a tiny abandoned fireplace, probably used by a former household servant. The first three stories of the Charlestown home were in the midst of renovation, transformed into condos, like so many in this old neighborhood of Boston. But the attic held clues to a different past, when Irish immigrant families had replaced the wealthy shipbuilders who had founded the neighborhood.

Liam glanced into the shadows behind airy cobwebs. Somewhere in the dark corners he knew there were bats waiting to swoop down on him. Hell, he hated bats. "Could it be any colder in here?"

"The presidential suite at the Four Seasons didn't happen to be on the right street," Sean muttered.

"I had a date tonight, you know. Cindy Wacheski was supposed to meet me at the pub at ten."

"You're going to run out of women in Boston to charm," Sean muttered.

"Luckily, new women arrive every day," Liam teased. "I could introduce you to a few, boyo. How long has it been?" He picked up the camera he had hanging from a strap around his neck, peered through the lens at his older brother and snapped the shutter. "You look like a guy who needs sex and a lot of it."

The flash illuminated the dark attic and Sean cursed vividly, holding his hand up to his eyes. "This is a stakeout. Anyone on the street can see that flash."

"I'm sure there are hordes of tourists on the street looking up at this place. I wouldn't be surprised if it was on the historic Boston tour." He shook his head in derision. "Couldn't you have found a place with heat? What could possibly be worth photographing in this attic?"

"It's not here. It's across the street. Take a look."

Liam reached down into his camera case and pulled out his telephoto lens, then exchanged it with the one on his camera. He walked to the grimy attic window and looked out at the street. To his eye, there wasn't anything worth watching outside. The sidewalk below was empty, the narrow street lined with parked cars.

"This is an important case," Sean said. "If you're in, you're in for good. No backing out later."

"You could at least start acting like you appreciate me more," Liam muttered. "I'm your brother and your roommate. I pay half the rent, and tidy up after you and collect your messages when you're out of town. I don't have to help you out with this case. I have important work of my own to do. What if I get an assignment from the *Globe*? Being a stringer means that I have to be available. I had a nice photo on page three of the sports section last week. Did you see it?"

"They pay you pennies. And you haven't paid the rent in three months."

"So, I'm a little short right now."

"If you do this job for me, I'll split my fee with you."

Sean had been working on and off as a private investigator for nearly four years, starting right after he'd washed out of the police academy—or, more accurately, got kicked out for chronic insubordination. Of the six brothers, Sean was the odd one, quiet, reserved and fiercely private. The only people he truly felt comfortable with were his brothers, and half the time they couldn't figure out what was going on in his head—especially in the past year or so.

Sean had built his business on tailing cheating spouses and deadbeat dads. He supplemented his income by tending bar at their father's South Boston pub. And when he needed help, he usually called on his little brother. Liam could always use an extra buck or two.

Sean made a perfect P.I. He was always silently watching those around him. Their eldest brother, Conor, was known as the steady one, and Dylan, the strong one. Brendan had always been a dreamer, an adventurer. Sean's twin, Brian, liked the spotlight, and was confident and gregarious.

And then there was Liam. His place in the family had been carved out early on. Liam was known simply as the charmer, the pretty boy who breezed through life with more friends and admirers than he could count. Though Liam had always considered his social skills rather ordinary, people just seemed to be drawn to him. Early on, he had learned how to read people.

He could see inside their heads and understand exactly what they wanted from him. And if he needed something in return, he would give them what they wanted. Sometimes it was nothing more than a smile or a compliment or simple reassurance. His brothers called it charm.

Maybe that's what made him a good photographer. He could look through a lens and see a story inside the people he photographed—all their fears and conflicts and doubts. He knew what the public wanted to see in a photograph and he gave that to them. Unfortunately the photo editors at the Boston *Globe* considered his work a bit too "artistic" for a daily newspaper. "Just give me a news photo," his editor would say, "not a damn masterpiece."

"So just how much am I going to make on this job?" Liam asked.

"We're working for a bank," Sean replied. "Management found a quarter million missing. They think a pair of employees embezzled it, then took off. After tracking one of them to Boston, they called me. If we find the money, we get ten percent."

Liam blinked in surprise. Split in two, that was over twelve thousand dollars! He barely made that in a year as a stringer. Twelve thousand would buy a lot of film and lab time. "Why don't they just call the police?"

"Bad P.R. for the bank. They brag about security on all their television commercials. It would look bad to admit the money is missing."

"All right. I'm in. What am I looking for?"

Sean stepped up to the window and pulled the

moth-eaten curtains back. "She lives there," he said, pointing to a window across the street.

"She?" Sean handed Liam a photo and he held it up to the light from a streetlamp outside. It revealed a rather plain-looking woman wearing glasses. Her hair was pulled back from her face and she wore a starched shirt with a scarf artfully tied at the neck. "She looks like my third-grade teacher, Miss Pruitt. We used to call her Miss Prunes."

"Eleanor Thorpe, twenty-six, graduated summa from Harvard business school. Took a job as an accountant at Intertel Bank in Manhattan right after graduation. Considered a stellar employee. Six weeks ago she quit without giving any reasons and showed up here in Boston. She's looking for another job in banking. She went back to Intertel for references."

"Isn't that a little odd for an embezzler to ask for references?" Liam questioned.

"It diverts suspicion. She lives there." He pointed in the direction of the place across the street. "Third floor in that redbrick, three-flat. All the windows are hers, bedroom on the right, living room on the left. Watch her, keep track of her visitors, keep a schedule of her movements." He handed Liam another photo, this time of a conservative-looking man. "Her partner, Ronald Pettibone, thirty-one, a co-worker at the bank. I want to know if he shows up. I need photos of them together."

"That's it? I'm just waiting for him?"

"Yep. If they were in it together, they should make contact so they can divide up the loot. When I get back from Atlantic City—"

"What's in Atlantic City?"

"A cheating husband," Sean said. "Big money and an infidelity clause in the prenup. She needs proof."

"Why don't you let me take that job and you can stay in this freezing attic and spy on the bean counter?"

"I wanna know who she sees, where she goes," Sean said.

"Why don't you just bug her apartment?"

"You can go to prison for that."

"And not for spying?"

"Nope."

"So, how long are you going to be gone? If I were going to Atlantic City, I'd have a little fun, meet some pretty girls, do a little gambling. I know this one lady down there who has a killer—"

"It's strictly business," Sean muttered.

Liam laughed. "It's hard to believe you're a Quinn. When they were handing out the hound-dog gene, they skipped over you."

"I don't spend every spare moment chasing woman," Sean murmured. "I have better things to do with my time."

"Hey, I don't chase women. They just happen to chase me. And why they keep chasing you, I'll never understand. Maybe they like that aloof, silent act of yours. Or maybe they enjoy the challenge. I can hardly wait for the Quinn curse to catch up to you."

"It won't if I stay away from women," Sean murmured. "You're the one who should worry."

Liam frowned. "I happen to love women. All kinds

of women. And if I keep moving from one to another, none of them will catch me."

Still, Liam's joking about the Quinn curse could only go so far. Throughout their childhood, their father had warned them of the dangers of love, hiding his own mistrust of women in the tales of the Mighty Quinns. But now that three of Seamus's sons had fallen under a woman's power, Seamus had declared that they'd been the victim of a long-ago curse.

He'd told the new tale to his sons one night when they were all gathered around the bar at the pub. And though the three oldest brothers scoffed at the idea, the three youngest weren't so skeptical. Liam wasn't about to be caught in the same trap that had caught Conor, Dylan and Brendan. In truth, he knew the secret, the reason Olivia, Meggie and Amy had managed to snare themselves a Quinn. "Never ride to the rescue of a damsel in distress," Liam murmured. For some reason, once a Quinn came to a woman's rescue, it seemed he was doomed.

He glanced down at his watch. Had this been a normal Friday night, he would have been behind the bar at Quinn's, scoping out the female clientele and deciding exactly which women he was going to charm that evening. Just because the three eldest Quinn brothers were off the market, women hadn't given up on the younger trio.

"I bought you beer and sandwiches," Sean said. "In the cooler. There's take-out Chinese just down the block. Coffee shop on the corner. If you need to leave, set up the video camera. I'll be back Sunday night, Monday night at the latest."

"What am I supposed to do if this guy shows up? Do I tail him or her?"

"Call me. You've got your cell phone and my number. Then get as much on him as you can, the make of his car, his plate number, anything that we can use to track him down. Hell, break into his car if you have to."

"Can't they put me in jail for that?" Liam asked with a grin.

"Only if you get caught," Sean said as he walked to the door.

Liam watched as his brother closed the attic door behind him, then turned back to the job at hand. Though the conditions weren't ideal, his side jobs for Sean were usually pretty easy. He turned back to the window and focused his telephoto lens on the third-floor apartment. The lights were on in all the rooms and he found the subject of their surveillance sitting in the living room. Her back was turned to Liam but he could tell she was reading a book.

Suddenly she stood, holding the book in one hand and gesturing wildly with the other. He quickly scanned the apartment, wondering who the hell she was talking to. Then he realized she was talking to herself. "Ground control, we have a loony here," he murmured.

Liam let the lens move along the length of her body. She was tall and slender with dark hair that fell to the middle of her back. A pair of faded jeans hugged her backside and her T-shirt was tight enough to reveal delicate shoulders and a narrow waist. "Come on, Eleanor," he murmured. "Turn around and give us a look. I'm not used to spending Friday night without some feminine companionship."

But she didn't turn. Instead she dropped her book and walked into the bedroom, too fast for him to focus on her face. When he caught her there again, Liam watched as she stood in front of the closet. Then, in one slow, sinuous movement, she grabbed the hem of her T-shirt and pulled it over her head. Liam held his breath for a moment, then let it out slowly. "Wow," he murmured.

Though he felt a bit like a peeping Tom, he couldn't drag himself away from the telephoto lens. He snapped a picture and the autowind on his camera whirred ahead to the next frame. "Turn around, turn around," he whispered.

But as if she were teasing him, she refused. Her jeans were next and she skimmed them off her hips and kicked them away. Dressed only in her bra and panties, she bent to pick up the jeans off the floor, offering Liam a tempting view of her backside. "Hmm, black underwear. Pretty racy for an accountant." He snapped another photo.

Suddenly the damp chill in the attic didn't seem to bother him. His blood pumped a little quicker, warmed by the subject in his viewfinder. He leaned forward, pressing the camera even closer to the grimy window. "Now the bra," he murmured. "Or the panties. I'm easy. You choose." And then she turned around and seemed to look directly at him, her dark hair tumbled around an exquisite face.

With a soft curse, Liam jumped back from the window, letting his camera drop against his chest. She was beautiful, nothing at all like the photo he'd been given. "Oh, hell," he muttered, raking his hand through his hair. He'd probably been watching the wrong window. He snatched up his camera and focused it on the building, counting the floors, reviewing the description his brother had given him.

But he was trained on the right place, and when he found her, she had turned again, reaching around for the hook on her bra. He swallowed hard. He'd been to strip clubs before and watched women take off their clothes for entertainment. But this was something more than just a gorgeous body, it was almost...intimate. And when she slipped into a silk robe, he breathed a long sigh of relief.

Who was this woman? She certainly wasn't the woman in the picture, all conservative and efficient-looking. But maybe that was all a part of it. Sean had said Eleanor Thorpe was a suspect in the embezzlement of a quarter-million dollars. What better way to pull off a crime like that than to play the part of the dependable, quietly forgettable employee?

She moved to the window. "No," he murmured. "Not the curtains. Leave them open." But his plea went unheard.

He dragged an old easy chair over to the window and sat, kicking his feet up on the sill. Liam watched the apartment for a long time, his mind spinning images of the woman inside. And when the lights of the apartment went off a few hours later, he took a long sip of the beer he'd opened.

Tipping his head back, he closed his eyes, ready to settle in for a long night. He saw her in his head, turning to face him, letting the silk robe drop to the floor. He imagined her body, perfect breasts, a slender waist, and long and supple legs. And then she began to move, a provocative dance caught by the lens of his camera.

Liam wasn't sure how long he'd slept or what woke him up—a noise from the street or maybe a sense of something happening. He rubbed his eyes, then looked at his watch. It was nearly midnight and the attic was frigid from the damp spring wind that had picked up outside.

He sat up and rubbed his arms, then raked his fingers through his hair. The apartment was still dark across the street, but he grabbed his camera and looked through the telephoto lens anyway. Somewhere in the distance a siren sounded, and nearby a dog barked. And then a strange light appeared in the window of Eleanor Thorpe's apartment.

Liam slowly stood and focused the lens. The light seemed as if it was coming from a moving source as it cast odd shadows against the living-room windows. "What the—" He adjusted the telephoto, searching, trying to see inside the darkened room. The light moved closer to the window and Liam realized that there was someone inside Eleanor Thorpe's apartment—someone dressed in black and carrying a flashlight.

"What the hell?"

Was this the man he was waiting for, Eleanor Thorpe's partner in crime? Or was Eleanor Thorpe about to become the victim of a burglary? Liam wasn't going to wait around to find out. As he ran to the door and raced down the stairs, he grabbed his cell phone from his pocket and dialed 9-1-1. "Burglary in progress," he said, bursting out the front door. "Six-seventeen Summer Street. Send a patrol car right away."

Liam found the front door of the three-flat ajar and he took the steps two at a time, trying to keep quiet as he approached. He knew that the police wouldn't arrive for at least a few minutes and hoped he wouldn't be facing some fool with a gun.

When he reached the third story, he slowly pushed the door open and allowed his eyes to adjust to the light. Then he saw him, a figure of average height and weight, moving around the living room, his face hidden by a ski mask. Liam took a deep breath, knowing it would take the element of surprise to subdue the guy. If he could just knock him off his feet, his greater height and weight would win out in the end.

He steeled his resolve and said a silent prayer that the guy didn't have a gun. Then he launched his body across the room, hitting the burglar square in the back and knocking him to the floor.

ELEANOR THORPE'S EYES opened suddenly and for a moment she wasn't sure where she was—or what had brought her out of a deep sleep. But when she heard a thud come from the vicinity of her living room, she bolted upright in her bed and wiped the sleep from her eyes.

She held her breath and waited, wondering if the sound came from the street. She'd locked the door before going to bed and she lived on the third floor, too high for someone to crawl in the window. But the back porch allowed easy access. After moving from Manhattan, she was well aware of the perils of city living. But there was no denying the fact that someone was in her apartment!

Her mind began to whirl with the possibilities. Should she call the police first and then try to lock her bedroom door? Or should she make sure of her safety first? She reached for her bedside table, then remembered that she didn't have a phone in her bedroom here, only in her old apartment in New York.

She slipped out of bed and tiptoed to the door. Only to realize it didn't have a lock! Now what? Ellie took a ragged breath. She had two choices—get to a phone or take her chances with whomever was banging around her living room. Well, three really. She could hide under the bed. Or scream until someone came to her rescue—that was four.

Gathering her courage, she started down the hall. As she stepped into the living room, she grabbed a lamp. Suddenly a figure appeared out of the dark. Ellie shrieked as loud as she could, then swung the lamp at his head. The ceramic base cracked and a soft curse slipped from the man's lips as he fell to his knees.

"Jeez, what the hell are you doing?" He rubbed his head. "That hurt!"

Ellie clutched the lamp tighter, determined this time to hit her mark. She raised it high. "Lie down on the floor and put your hands behind your head."

"What?" He cursed again. "I came in here to—"

"Do it," she threatened. "Or I'll knock you senseless."

"I'm not the one," he said, feebly pointing across the living room. "It was him."

Ellie glanced in the direction he pointed and noticed a dark figure crawling along the floor toward the open door of her apartment. Her first instinct was to find another lamp and throw it at his head. But she already had one of the burglars subdued. With his help, the police would be able to track down the other.

She caught movement from the corner of her eye just in time to find the man at her feet making a lunge for her waist. With a tiny cry of alarm, she brought the remains of the lamp crashing down on his head. He hit the floor with a thud as the other intruder stumbled down the stairs. Taking in another ragged breath, Ellie hurried over to the light switch and flipped it on.

The man lying on her Oriental rug didn't look nearly as frightening as he had in the dark. She gave him a poke with her toe just to make sure he was out, then raced through the apartment to find something to bind his hands and feet. Plastic wrap and a few pair of panty hose would have to do.

She quickly trussed him up like a Thanksgiving turkey, sitting on the small of his back as she tied his feet to his hands. Then she sighed softly and began to search his pockets for some kind of identification. If he managed to escape, at least she'd have his name.

He groaned softly and Ellie jumped away from him, retreating across the room. She grabbed up the phone and dialed 9-1-1. "I'm calling the police," she shouted. "Don't try to escape."

"Don't bother," he muttered. "I already called them on my way over here."

"What do you mean?"

"I was here to help. I saw that guy breaking into your apartment, so I followed him in."

Ellie frowned. "I don't believe you."

"Fine," he said. "Let the cops sort it out."

The emergency operator answered and Ellie quickly gave her the address, only to learn that the police were already on their way. Ellie informed them that she'd tied up the burglar and he'd be waiting for the police when they arrived. Then she hung up and watched her captive. Deciding she'd need another weapon, she ran to the kitchen and retrieved the biggest knife she could find. She perched on the arm of the sofa and watched him warily.

The burglar winced as he shifted, trying to get comfortable. "These knots are a little tight."

"Shut up," she said.

A long silence grew between them. Ellie tried to slow her pounding heart and replenish her courage.

"So what do you think he was after?" the burglar murmured.

"Who?"

"The guy you let get away. Is anything missing? When I came in, he was going through your desk. Do you keep money in there?"

"I'm not telling you where I keep my money," Ellie said. For a criminal he was awfully concerned about her welfare. A guy so handsome shouldn't have to make his living on the other side of the law. She opened his wallet and began to flip through it. "So...Liam Quinn, what made you turn to a life of crime?"

"What makes you so sure I'm a criminal?"

Ellie wasn't sure. But what choice did she have? Criminals weren't known to be the most honest people in the world. She wasn't about to fall for some line. "If you're not a criminal, then what are you?"

"A photographer," he said. "I string for the *Globe* and one of the news syndicates. There's a clipping tucked in my wallet, next to the money. That was the first photo I had published."

She pulled out the folded newspaper and smoothed it on her knee. It was a photo of a little girl dressed in a huge firefighter's jacket, clutching a ragged teddy bear. Her gaze dropped to the credit line. "Photo by Liam Quinn."

"I took that three years ago. Her house burned in a fire. Her family lost everything."

"She looks so sad," Ellie murmured.

"Yeah. She was. But that photo caused a lot of publicity for the family. People sent money, and by the end of the week there was a fund established to help her family replace everything they'd lost. I felt like I'd done a good thing." He twisted and sighed impatiently. "Can you just loosen my feet? I've got a cramp in my thigh that's killing me. I promise I won't try to run."

Ellie hesitated, glancing down at the photo. She riffled through the rest of his wallet. She found a press pass for the Boston *Globe*, three credit cards and punch card for a place called Cuppa Joe's. She also found a small photo of a family at a wedding, an elderly couple standing next to a beautiful bride and handsome groom. They were flanked by six tall, dark and hand-some men. One was Liam Quinn.

This didn't add up. He looked like such a nice guy. Maybe he *was* only trying to help. "I have a knife," she said. "And I want you to stay on the floor."

"Deal," he said.

Ellie approached him and untied his feet. Then she stepped back. He rolled onto his back and wriggled over to the sofa, then leaned back against it. For the first time she got a good look at his face and she real-ized that the picture of him in his wallet didn't do him justice. He was most likely the most gorgeous man, criminal or not, that she'd ever set eyes on. And he also had a cut on his forehead that was dripping blood.

"You're hurt," she murmured.

"I'm not surprised," he said with a chuckle. "You hit me pretty hard."

Ellie knew she shouldn't trust him, but he seemed content to wait for the police. She got up from the sofa and backed toward the kitchen. "Don't move." She quickly grabbed the box of bandages from the drawer beside the sink, then wet a wad of paper towel. When she returned to the living room, he was right where she'd left him.

"I'm going to bandage the cut on your forehead. If you even twitch, I'll stab you with this knife. Under-stood?"

"Understood."

She knelt beside him, setting the knife next to her on the floor. Then she leaned close and dabbed at the cut with the damp paper towel. "It doesn't look too bad," she said. "I don't think it will need stitches."

He winced as she pressed on the cut to slow the bleeding. "I didn't twitch," he said. "That was just a reaction to pain."

Ellie let her gaze drift down to his eyes, an odd mixture of green and gold. She stared at him for a long moment, her heart skipping a beat. She saw no evil in his gaze, no malicious intent. Instead she saw warmth and—amusement?

"Stop it," she murmured.

"What?"

"Nothing," Ellie said. This was what always got her in trouble! She'd encounter an attractive man and, before she knew anything about him, she'd fabricate a wildly romantic and dashing personality for him. She just loved being in love. It was like a sickness. In fact she'd just read a self-help book, *Loving Out Loud*, that advised a daily reality check when it came to romance. "Fracture the fairy tale," the author had written.

Love had been precisely the thing that had sent her running from New York and a job she'd adored. Actually, it wasn't love, but the lack of love. Not on her side, but on— She cursed inwardly. Ellie had vowed never to speak or think his name again. All right, Ronald Pettibone. When she'd first met him, she'd thought his name was so aristocratic. And he had a nose to match his name. And then she'd—

"Maybe you should call the police again," Liam said. "They're taking a long time to respond to a 9-1-1. I could have had a gun. You could be lying dead in the middle of this room right now. My brother is a cop, and I understand what kind of pressure they're under, but this is ridiculous. My hands are starting to fall asleep."

"I suppose I could untie you and you could—" She hesitated. "No. No, no, no. I'm doing it again. I can't believe this. After Ronald, I swore off men and now—" Ellie ground her teeth. "You're very nice-looking. I'm sure you know that. And if you did save my life, I'm grateful. But I've been entirely too trusting when it comes to men and that's got to stop. Right now."

Liam frowned. "Who's Ronald?"

"None of your business!"

"Hey, I'm just making conversation, Eleanor."

Ellie frowned. "How did you know my name?"

He paused for a moment. "You gave it to the police when you called."

"I said Ellie."

"I assumed Ellie was short for Eleanor. Isn't it? Or are you Ellen? Eloise? Elfreida?"

She tore the wrapping off the bandage and quickly covered the cut. "Ellie. That's all you need to know."

"And who's Ronald?"

Ellie sat back on her heels and picked up the knife again. "My ex-boyfriend. But I don't want to talk about him. In fact, I don't think we should be talking at all."

"We could always talk about you."

Ellie wagged her finger at him. "Oh, no. Don't try to turn on the charm. I'm not going to fall for that. I'm impervious. I'm a rock."

He chuckled softly. "All right. Then maybe you could get me a glass of water. I'm a little—"

The thud of footsteps on the stairs interrupted his request and Ellie jumped up, anxious to put as much space as she could between her and Liam Quinn. He was exactly the kind of man she always fell for. In truth, he was a whole lot nicer looking than the men in her past. And if he really was a photographer, then he was probably a lot more interesting, as well. And he had a better body and a decent fashion sense. And he knew how to choose men's cologne.

"Police!"

Ellie turned to the door, setting the knife on a nearby table. The two officers rushed into the room, their guns drawn. Ellie sat on the sofa and watched as they patted Liam down and pulled him to his feet. Then they shoved him up against the wall and searched him more thoroughly.

"Would you like to tell us what you were doing in this lady's apartment?"

"I was passing by on the street and I saw an intruder slip in the front door."

"Yeah, right. How did you know it was an intruder and not this lady's husband?"

"Oh, I'm not married," Ellie piped up.

"He was wearing a ski mask," Liam explained. "I figured my first impression was probably right. Hey, we can clear this all up right now if you just call the downtown station house. My brother is a detective there. Conor Quinn."

They turned him around. "We're from the downtown precinct," the taller officer said, "and I don't know any detective named—"

"I do," the other officer said. "Conor Quinn. He's in homicide. Tall, dark-haired guy. Wife just had a baby. In fact, this guy looks a lot like him."

"She's got my ID," Liam said, nodding toward Ellie.

Ellie quickly stood and handed the officer Liam's wallet. "He's telling the truth. His name is Liam Quinn and he's a photographer. And—and I think I may have made a mistake."

The short officer cuffed Liam and shoved him toward the door. "I'll take him down to the car while you take her statement," he said.

"'Bye!" Ellie called as Liam walked through the door. "It was nice meeting you." She paused. "Officer, can you make sure you have a doctor look at the cut on his forehead? It could need stitches."

"Ma'am, why don't you have a seat and we'll figure out what happened here?" the officer suggested.

"All right. But I want you to know that he was very polite and well behaved while he was here. And he told the truth. There was someone else in the apartment. I saw him run out. I thought they were partners. I didn't realize he was trying to save me."

"What his intentions were aren't really clear, ma'am. I just need your side of the story."

Ellie folded her hands on her lap and began to recount the events of that night from the moment she woke up. As she did, her mind kept returning to the instant her eyes had met Liam's, to the powerful current that had passed between them. Had she simply imagined it or was the attraction mutual? As she spoke she tried to push the thought from her head.

For all she knew he was a burglar and he'd end up in prison for his crime. But in her heart she hoped it wasn't true. She hoped that the story he'd told was real, that a handsome stranger had come to her rescue without thought to his own safety.

"Is Liam Quinn going to go to jail?" she asked.

"Do you want him to go to jail?" the officer countered.

"I really think he was telling the truth. If you think he's telling the truth, then you should let him go."

"Is anything missing?"

Ellie glanced around. "Liam said the guy was going through my desk when he came in. But there's nothing of value there. My computer is still here and so is the television and the stereo equipment."

"Well, if you find anything missing, call me and I'll put it into the report." The officer handed her a business card as he stood. "And you may want to get those locks checked. Burglars sometimes come back a second time."

Ellie showed the policeman to the door, then closed it behind him, making sure to lock the dead bolt. Then she grabbed up the knife and sat on the sofa. She was afraid to go to bed now, afraid that whoever had broken in would come back. She scrambled off the sofa and picked up a chair from the dining alcove, then jammed it under the doorknob. But, given the choice, she didn't want to depend upon locks and chairs and butcher knives to protect herself.

A lot of good her white knight was doing her now, locked up in a jail cell. "I should have left him tied up on the floor," Ellie said. But somehow she suspected that he wouldn't have stayed tied up for long. Liam Quinn would have convinced her to untie him—and then who knows what might have happened?

2

LIAM LAY on the cold steel bench in the holding cell.
Until a few moments ago, the cell had been filled with
an assortment of petty criminals—two pimps, a handful of drunk and disorderlies, and four Harvard boys
who'd been caught trying to climb the steeple of the
Old South Meeting House. But they'd all been hustled
out to central booking and then to night court, leaving
Liam to the rather Spartan and smelly accommoda-
tions.

This was all his fault. He'd spent too much time listening to those stupid Mighty Quinn stories when he
was a kid and the first chance he had, he decided to
ride to the rescue. He could have waited for the police
or alerted a neighbor or even caused enough commo-
tion on the street to send the guy running. But instead
he'd felt compelled to burst into Eleanor Thorpe's
apartment to snatch her from the jaws of certain danger.

His mind flashed an image of her dressed in the
nearly transparent nightgown. Once she'd turned on
the light in the living room, he could see right through
the thin cotton.

Liam groaned and put his arm over his eyes, trying
to banish the image from his head. But it lingered in
his mind, and rather than fight it, Liam decided to en-

joy it. She had incredibly long legs, slender and perfectly shaped, and hips that curved in a way that made her seem instantly seductive. And her breasts—her breasts were just... Liam swallowed hard, his fingers clenching into fists.

Hell, it wasn't as if she was the prettiest woman he'd ever seen. Not even close. In truth, her features just weren't that remarkable. Though she did have very nice eyes, her mouth was just a little too wide, her lips too lush. And her dark hair fell around her face in a way that made her look as if she'd just gotten out of bed—which she had.

As he thought about their encounter, he realized it was more than her looks that attracted him. But what was it? Was it the breathless way she spoke when she was nervous? Or the way she moved, almost amusing in her awkwardness?

Maybe it was the fact that she'd never once responded to him the way other women had. She hadn't cozied up to him and found any excuse she could to touch him. She hadn't sent him teasing looks or seductive smiles. No, Ellie Thorpe had hit him over the head with a lamp then tied him up like some S & M fantasy man. And even after he was certain he'd convinced her of his innocence, she still hadn't fallen prey to his charms.

"I just wasn't trying hard enough," Liam murmured.

A cell door slammed nearby and Liam glanced up to find a uniformed officer watching him from behind steel bars. He quickly stood and crossed the cell. "Can I have my phone call?"

"You had your phone call," the officer said.

Liam had decided Conor was his only option when it came to straightening out this mess. But the late-night call had been answered not by Conor or Olivia, but by their voice mail, and Liam had hung up without leaving a message. "I couldn't get hold of my brother. It doesn't count if I didn't talk to anyone."

"Are you making the rules now, Quinn?"

Liam shook his head. "No, I'm just saying that—"

"You got caught breaking and entering. Right about now, you should be sitting in night court and thinking about how you're going to make bail."

Liam pressed his forehead against the cold, steel bars. "This isn't exactly the way I wanted to spend my Friday night. I had a date that I canceled. I should have just gone on that date and not even bothered saving Eleanor Thorpe's life. You'd think she'd be at least a little grateful."

The cop reached down and unlocked the cell door. "Well, I guess she was. Her story checked with yours. And we paged your brother. He's downstairs talking to the two guys who arrested you."

"I'm free to go?"

"We're not booking you. But that doesn't mean you shouldn't try to keep your nose clean. The next time you see someone breaking and entering, dial 9-1-1 and wait for the police."

Liam smiled. "Right. That's exactly what I'll do. By the book next time. I promise."

The cop swung open the door, waiting for Liam. Without wasting any time, Liam grabbed his jacket and walked toward the exit. But at the last moment he turned and took one long, last look. There were times when he wondered just what kind of guardian angel sat on his shoulder. His childhood hadn't exactly been the best in the world. There's no telling what kind of wrong turn he might have taken had he made just one or two bad decisions.

But instead of a life as a petty criminal, he'd actually survived a shaky childhood and become a responsible adult. The kind of adult who'd try to save a woman from an intruder. Maybe the Mighty Quinn tales had done some good—not that he was planning to take up a career as a superhero.

Liam followed the cop to the door of the holding area. "He's downstairs at the desk," the officer said. "You need to sign for your stuff."

"Thanks."

Liam saw Conor before he even reached the bottom of the stairs. His big brother stood below, his eyes dark with anger, his arms crossed over his chest. Liam grinned as he hurried down the steps, but he could tell that Conor was in a foul mood.

"Hey, bro," he said, giving his brother a playful clap on the shoulder. "I knew I could count on you."

"Don't say a word," Conor warned. "The next thing out of your mouth better be an apology or I'll take you out back and beat the crap out of you."

"Sorry," Liam murmured. "I didn't know who else to call."

Conor turned on his heel and strode to the door, nodding brusquely to the desk sergeant as he passed. "Thanks, Willie. I owe you."

When they reached Conor's car, Liam slipped in the

passenger side, watching in silence as his brother pulled out into traffic. "My car is in Charlestown. If you could just drop me—"

"I'm not taking you to get your car. You can do that in the morning."

"Where are we going?"

"To Da's place."

"Good," Liam said. "I could use a drink."

"I'm going to have the drink and you're going to explain why you got me out of bed at one a.m. on a Friday night. Since Riley was born, Olivia and I have averaged about three hours of sleep a night, and when my beeper went off, he woke up and started crying."

"How is the kid?" Liam asked.

"Probably still awake. He's either sleeping or eating. And when he isn't doing one or the other, he cries. Olivia is exhausted."

The mood in the car remained tense and Liam was glad when they finally reached the pub. Friday night business had always been good in Southie, and the bar was still packed when they walked inside. Two pretty girls sitting at the bar called Liam's name as he entered and he waved, trying to remember their names. He found himself comparing their rather conspicuous beauty to the subtle attractions of Eleanor Thorpe.

She wasn't pretty in the traditional sense. She didn't have pouty lips or sultry eyes or a body designed for a men's magazine. In truth, she was the exact opposite of the type of woman he was drawn to—a little uptight, a little goofy. But there was something about her that he found undeniably attractive.

Maybe it was the fact that she'd single-handedly

subdued an intruder. She hadn't cowered in a corner or locked herself in the bathroom, she'd picked up a lamp and hit him over the head. Liam rubbed his wrists, still chafed from the ties. She hadn't known who he was or what his intent had been. For all she'd known, he could have been a crazed serial killer out to do her harm, but she'd stood up for herself.

Seamus, tending bar, drew two pints of Guinness and set them down in front of his sons as they each took an empty stool at the far end of the bar. "Didn't expect to see you out tonight, Con." He turned to Liam, his snow-white hair falling across his forehead. "As for you, I could have used your help behind the bar, boyo. Your brother Brian was the only relief I had and he left an hour ago with a blonde. And where the hell is Sean when I need him?"

"He's out of town," Liam said.

Seamus shrugged, then wandered off to talk with another customer.

Conor took a slow sip of his Guinness, then licked his upper lip. "What were you doing in that woman's apartment?"

"Exactly what I told the police. I was trying to protect her."

Conor slowly shook his head. "Go back to the beginning."

"I saw this guy sneak inside her apartment."

"From the street?"

"No, from the attic of the building across the street."

"And what were you doing in the—" Conor paused. "Don't tell me. You were on a case with Sean, weren't you? You know damn well that he skirts the law every chance he gets. What was this, another one of his divorce cases?''

''Well, as Sean would say, his clients expect a high level of confidentiality. All I can say is that I was watching the apartment. I told the cop I was walking by and he bought the story. As long as you vouch for me, I think I'll be all right.''

''Did you get a look at the burglar?''

Liam shook his head. ''Nah, it was dark and he was wearing a ski mask. He wasn't very tall. About five-eight or nine, maybe. Not very heavy. And he was kind of clumsy. Not much of a street fighter. I told this all to the cops.''

''You're not going to tell me what kind of case you and Sean are working on?''

''I think it would be better if you don't ask. And we haven't broken any laws—not yet, anyway. I swear.''

Conor rubbed his forehead. ''And except for the reason you were on the street, did you tell the police the entire truth?''

''Yeah.''

Conor nodded. ''Fine. As long as the woman doesn't insist on pressing charges, I think you'll be all right.''

''Eleanor. Ellie Thorpe. She's really nice. Kind of goofy, but nice.''

Conor's brow shot up. ''What? You had a conversation?''

''Well, there wasn't much else to do once she tied me up. It took the police forever to arrive.''

This brought a laugh from Conor. ''Jeez, Liam. You break into a woman's house, she ties you up, and you still manage to charm her. Did you get her phone number?"

"No," Liam replied. He shrugged, then smiled. "But I know where she lives."

Conor took a long drink of his beer, then slid off the bar stool and grabbed his keys. "You know what this means, don't you? When a Quinn rescues a woman from harm, he's pretty much done for. You're stuck with her now, Li. There's no going back."

"You don't think I believe all that Mighty Quinn garbage, do you?" Liam said. "I did a good deed and that's the end of it. I'm never going to see her again."

Liam wasn't afraid of being vulnerable to love. Hell, he knew better. He'd always been the one to walk away from a relationship when it got too serious. Besides, he wasn't about to get involved with a probable felon.

"Stay away from her," Conor warned. "She might just decide to press charges and I only have so much juice with the guys downtown." He sighed. "By the way, we're having a little get-together for Riley's christening. A brunch. Olivia sent you an invitation. Did you get it?"

"Yeah. I thought I'd stop by. Who else will be there?"

"Everyone."

"Ma, too?"

"Of course," Conor said. "She *is* Riley's grand-mother. And Olivia's parents are coming up from Florida."

Since Fiona had reappeared in their lives over a year ago, family gatherings had become regularly scheduled events. First, there'd been Keely's wedding, and after that a birthday celebration for Seamus held at Quinn's Pub. And last May, Dylan and Meggie's wedding. And then Christmas at Keely and Rafe's. And everyone had gathered at the hospital the night Riley was born, a large, noisy family still learning how to be a family.

Even though Liam's father was gradually making peace with his runaway wife, not all the old scars had healed. Conor had accepted his mother back with no questions asked, as had Dylan and Brian. But Brendan had maintained a cool distance and Sean was outright hostile toward Fiona. Liam wasn't sure where he stood yet. Though he wanted to get to know his mother, he had no past to remember. She'd left when he was just a year old.

"I'll be there," Liam said.

"Good. And see if you can convince Sean to come. Don't tell him Fiona is going to be there, though. Oh, and bring your camera."

"Anything else?"

"Just be sure you stay out of trouble until then."

"Hey, you won't mention this to Sean, will you? He's paying me pretty well to help with this case. I could use the money."

Conor smiled. "No problem." With that, he turned and strode out of Quinn's Pub, Seamus shouting a hearty good-night.

Liam finished his beer, then followed Conor out the door. He zipped up his jacket and glanced up and down the street. He and Sean had a flat seven blocks from the bar. He could go home and get some sleep or he could go back to the attic and keep his eye on Ellie Thorpe.

Liam shook his head as he headed for the bus stop. He wasn't going back for *her.* He had a job to do and he promised Sean he'd do it. The fact that he hadn't been able to get Ellie out of his head since he'd met her made absolutely no difference at all.

"DOUBLE AMERICANO, half caf!"

A man in a business suit pushed past Ellie to retrieve his coffee from the counter. Ellie raked her fingers through her hair and yawned. She leaned over and counted the number of people in front of her, deciding she'd get four shots of espresso in her latte rather than her usual two. Since her encounter with Liam Quinn three nights ago, she really hadn't gotten a good night's sleep.

Her mind flashed back to a memory of him tied up on her living-room floor. A tiny flush warmed her cheeks. She certainly hadn't expected her next encounter with a handsome man to include a little bondage. Just the thought of indulging in sex games with a man like Liam Quinn was enough to start her blood pumping much more effectively than any form of caffeine could.

Luckily, the police had dragged him away before she'd had more serious thoughts in that direction. When she'd left New York City, she'd vowed to take a break from men. It wasn't that she didn't like men, they just never seemed to like her—enough. She'd had five serious relationships in as many years and all of them had fallen apart for reasons unknown to her.

One day everything had been perfect and the next she'd been single again.

After the second breakup, Ellie had decided that men were just fickle. After the third, she'd determined that she'd have to be more careful with her choices. By the fourth, she'd started to wonder if there was something wrong with her. And after her breakup with Ronald Pettibone, she'd come to the conclusion that she just wasn't any good at romance.

Ronald had been a quiet, unassuming man with nothing in his life except his job at the bank. He didn't watch ESPN, didn't drink or smoke, and didn't even have any male friends. And from the moment they'd met, he'd only had eyes for her. Ellie had been sure she'd finally found a man worth loving. And then, again, it was suddenly over with no explanation. Working with him had been unbearable, so she'd decided to leave New York to make a fresh start in Boston.

But she hadn't expected to be quite so lonely. She didn't know a soul in the city, and without a new job, she had no way to make friends. The only person who ever recognized her was the curly-haired girl who took her coffee order every morning. "Large latte with four shots of caf, Erica," Ellie said with a bright smile.

Erica gave her an odd look, as if trying to place her face. "That'll be four fifty-six, ma'am."

Ellie glanced up at the clock. It was only seven, two hours earlier than she usually began her day. Maybe Erica wasn't used to seeing her so early. Ellie made a note to reread *I'm the Best Me I Can Be*, her favorite book of positive affirmations. She had four interviews set up with Boston banks this week alone and it wouldn't do to let the coffee girl shake her confidence.

She pulled her wallet out of her purse. She'd already interviewed for six other jobs and found it strange that she hadn't been called back by anyone. Though she'd left her job in New York rather suddenly, she'd left on good terms. Her old boss had no reason to give her anything but a glowing recommendation. Ellie sighed. Maybe the job market was just a little tight.

Ellie paid for her latte, then grabbed the paper cup and carried it over to the table that held the cream and sugar. She plucked a plastic top from a stack and before putting it onto the cup, sprinkled two packets of sugar into the coffee. When she was satisfied that her coffee was perfect, she turned for the door, then stopped short. The subject of her sleepless dreams stood at the end of the coffee line, his hands shoved into the pockets of his faded jeans, his broad shoulders accented by his battered leather jacket.

She looked over at the door and wondered if she ought to just walk out. He hadn't noticed her yet and she could easily make an escape. But Ellie felt compelled to say something to him. She owed him at least a thank-you, some acknowledgment that he'd likely saved her life.

She stepped up behind him and gave him a gentle tap on the shoulder. He slowly turned and Ellie found her heart fluttering as he looked into her eyes. She was struck again by the incredible color of his eyes, an odd mix of green and gold. She swallowed hard. "Hello," Ellie murmured.

Liam blinked, obviously surprised by her sudden appearance. "Hello," he said.

He gave her an odd look, the same look Erica had given her, and for a moment Ellie wondered if he remembered who she was. Her stomach lurched and she forced a smile. "It's Ellie," she explained. "Eleanor Thorpe. From—"

"I know," Liam said. "I know who you are. It's a little hard to forget the woman who tied me up and had me arrested."

"I'm sorry," Ellie said. "I called the police station Saturday morning and they explained everything. That you weren't a burglar or even a criminal. And that you were really coming to my rescue. I guess I ought to thank you."

He glanced around nervously, then fixed his gaze on the menu above the counter. Ellie wondered why he was being so aloof. Was he embarrassed by what she'd done? Or was he simply not interested in chit-chat? He'd been so charming that night and now he seemed as if he wanted to be anywhere but here talking with her. "Well, I should really go."

"Right," he murmured. "You know, I really didn't save you. The guy probably was just after some jewelry or maybe some easy cash."

"No, no, you did," Ellie insisted. "The desk sergeant told me I was very lucky you came along. Burglars often come armed and if I had caught him in my apartment, he probably would have shot me. So you were like a…a white knight."

"No, I wasn't," Liam said. "Not even close."

An uneasy silence grew between them and Ellie

shrugged casually. "Well, I guess I should get going. Thanks again."

"No problem," Liam said.

Ellie hesitantly started toward the door, then stopped short. This was crazy. She didn't have a single friend in Boston and Liam Quinn had been the very first interesting person she'd met. Even though he was a man and she'd sworn off men for at least the next year, she could at least try to get to know him a little better as a friend.

Ellie turned and walked back to him, taking a deep breath and gathering her courage. "Would you like to have dinner with me?" The words came out before she realized she was talking to his back. She quickly circled him to stand within his line of sight. "Would you like to have dinner with me?"

"Me?"

"I feel as if I should do something for you. As a gesture of gratitude."

"It wasn't really any big deal."

Ellie frowned. "Is there some reason why you don't like me?"

"I don't know you," Liam said.

"You seem to be a little nervous around me. Is it because I tied you up? If I'd known you were trying to help, I wouldn't have done that." She cleared her throat. "I'm not one of those women who feels compelled to dominate men. I hit you on the head because I was scared and I tied you up because I didn't want you to get away."

"I understand."

"Good. I'm glad we got that straight." She swallowed hard then pasted a bright smile on her face. "Well, I should really be going. It was nice seeing you again. Good luck with your photography."

Ellie quickly turned on her heel and headed for the door, certain she'd made a complete ass of herself. She knew enough about men to know when one wasn't interested. Liam Quinn couldn't have been more indifferent. Maybe she gave off some kind of strange aura that men found repulsive. The author of *What Men Really Think,* the book she'd read after her breakup with Ronald, claimed that a woman uninterested in a relationship gave off subtle clues to her indifference that only a man could read.

"Ellie?"

She stopped and glanced over her shoulder at Liam. "Yes?"

"I'd love to have dinner. When?"

"How...how about tonight?"

"Tonight would be great. What time?"

"Seven?"

Liam nodded. "I'll see you then. I know where you live."

Ellie smiled, then hurried out the door before he could reconsider. For the first time since she'd come to Boston, she felt as if she might like it here. She'd made one friend and even though he was just about the sexiest guy she'd ever laid eyes on, she was simply going to enjoy the acquaintance and not worry about romance.

When she reached the street, she glanced back, hoping to catch one last look at him. But when she turned around to continue her walk home, she bumped into a man on the sidewalk. They both stopped and Ellie looked at him and gasped.

"Ronald?"

"Eleanor? What are you doing here?"

She stared up into the face of the man who'd once been her lover. "Me? I live here now." He looked completely different. His usually tidy hair, mussed by the wind, was much longer than she remembered and it looked as if he'd had it highlighted. And he wasn't wearing glasses. And his pasty complexion was perfectly bronzed. "I barely recognize you. What are you doing in Boston?"

"This is incredible. You're the last person I expected to see today."

"Then you're not here to see me?"

"No," Ronald said. "I didn't even know you were here. I'm visiting an old college buddy from Columbia. He lives a few blocks from here. I was just looking for a good cup of coffee." He paused. "But maybe it's fate we ran into each other. I've been thinking about you lately," he said, running his hand along her arm, "wondering how you've been doing."

"I've been doing fine, Ronald," Ellie replied, not willing to give him any encouragement. To her surprise, she felt no attraction to him at all. His touch left her cold. At the time of their breakup, she'd wondered if she'd ever get over him. At least she had her answer.

"We should get together," Ronald suggested. "What are you doing tonight?"

Ellie sighed softly. "Ronald, I've started a new life here. What we had didn't work out and I've moved on. I think you should, too. It was good to see you again, but I have to go now."

He grabbed her wrist and yanked her to a stop. "Come on, Eleanor. Don't be that way. We can still be friends."

"You dumped me, Ronald. You asked me to give back the pearl necklace you bought me for my birthday and the music box you gave me to put it in. And then you paraded your new girlfriend around the bank just a week after we broke up. I don't think we can be friends."

"Don't say that!" he said, anger lacing his tone. "There's no reason we can't—"

"No!" Ellie cried, twisting out of his grip.

"Is everything all right here?"

Ronald looked up, his hand falling to his side. Ellie had never realized how short Ronald was, or how skinny. Compared to Liam Quinn, he looked almost wimpy. "I'm fine," she said.

"I—I gotta go," Ronald said. "I'll see you around."

He hurried off and Ellie watched him as he disappeared around the corner. Then she turned back to Liam Quinn. "Thanks."

"Who was that guy?"

"No one."

He searched her face, as if he didn't believe her. "It looked like he was angry with you."

"No, we barely know each other."

"What did he want?"

Ellie smiled. "Nothing. Just wanted to say hello. Really, I'm fine."

"Good," Liam said. "Then I guess I'll see you tonight."

As he walked off in the opposite direction, Ellie headed toward her apartment. She fought the impulse to look back, knowing that she didn't want to appear completely enthralled with him. But when she rounded the corner, she stopped and looked back down the street. Liam was gone. Ellie smiled. At least, this time, she knew her white knight would return.

ELLIE LIFTED THE LID from the pasta pot, then glanced up at the clock on the kitchen wall. They'd agreed on a time for dinner, but she didn't know whether Liam Quinn would expect to eat the moment he walked in or if he'd want to socialize for a while.

When she'd invited him to dinner, it had been an impulsive move. Once she'd had a chance to think about it, she realized that the "date" raised all sorts of problems. Should they go out to dinner or stay in? If they went out, would he insist on paying? Since she'd invited him, the choice of restaurant would be up to her. And she wasn't yet familiar with many places in Boston. No, she'd made the best decision. She'd prepare a lovely meal at her apartment—and then she'd have him all to herself, with no distractions.

"Don't do this!" Ellie muttered, letting the lid drop back onto the pot with a clatter. She brushed her hair back from her eyes, then strode into the living room. She found the book open on her coffee table and picked it up. She'd purchased *Making Friends with Men* just that afternoon, determined not to fall into the same old traps again.

The author wrote quite eloquently about the rewards of male-female friendships, but warned that the moment romance crept into the relationship, it was usually ruined for good. If Ellie hadn't had such a lousy track record with men, then maybe she would have considered a romance with Liam Quinn. But she was at a point in her life when she needed a friend more than she needed a lover.

"Oh, who are you kidding!" She slapped the book shut and picked up another. *Be Honest with Yourself: A Guide to Awareness.* Dr. Dina Sanders claimed the most dangerous flaw a person could possess was self-delusion. And if Ellie didn't acknowledge that Liam was the sexiest hunk of man she'd ever met, then she was the queen of self-denial.

"All right, he's sexy. That face is just too pretty for words and he's got gorgeous eyes and a smile that could make a girl melt. And his body is to die for. I'll admit that. When he moves, I just want to watch him and think about him naked. He's a fine specimen of a man." Ellie stopped, then reconsidered what she'd said. A giggle slipped from her lips and she tossed the book back onto the coffee table.

"Don't look for the answers in a book," she murmured. "Look in your heart." That's what psychologist Jane Fleming had said in her book, *Listen to Your Heart.* Though at the time Ellie had thought it was a bit of a paradox, considering that advice came from a book. Still, it was good advice.

"I'll just follow my heart," she said. "But I'll make sure I listen to my brain, as well."

A raucous buzz broke the silence in the apartment

and Ellie jumped, pressing her hand to her chest. Beneath her fingers she could feel her heart racing. Inhaling a deep breath, she tried to calm herself. "No pressure, this is just a friendly dinner." So why had she spent nearly two hours on her hair and makeup? "A very friendly dinner."

She pressed the security buzzer, then opened her door and waited for him to climb the two flights up to her apartment. When he rounded the landing, she noticed that he was carrying a lamp. At that moment he saw her and their eyes met, and for a second Ellie couldn't breathe. Why did he seem to get more handsome each time she saw him?

"Hi," she murmured. "You brought a lamp."

"This is for you," Liam said.

She stepped aside to let him walk into the apartment, then softly closed the door behind him, taking just a moment to stare at his backside. "Thank you. But you didn't have to."

"I know guys usually bring flowers or candy. But I figured after you broke your lamp on my head, I owed you one."

Ellie grinned and reached for it. "Thanks. I'll just go put it in water."

That brought a smile to Liam's lips. "I'll just go plug it in." He fished a light bulb out of the pocket of his leather jacket. "I thought about getting you a lamp with a brass base, but I figured if you ever decided to hit me again, I didn't want to end up in the hospital."

"How is your head?"

"I had a small lump, but it's going down."

She felt a warm blush creep up her cheeks. "I really do apologize."

He glanced over at her. "Hey, there's no need. You did what you had to do."

Ellie pointed to the far wall. "There's a plug behind the sofa."

Liam set the lamp on the table, then shrugged out of his jacket, revealing a finely pressed shirt that accented his wide shoulders and narrow waist. Ellie quickly hurried across the room and took his jacket from him. "I'll just throw this in my bedroom." Right after she said it, Ellie realized that he might misunderstand. "Not that I expect us to end up in the—it's just that I don't have a coat closet in this apartment. These old places are—"

"You can put my coat on your bed," Liam said. "I'm sure it won't get any ideas."

Ellie stifled a groan, then hurried to her bedroom. She sat on the edge of her bed, clutching his coat to her chest. "Be cool," she murmured. "Just be cool." She lifted his jacket to her face and buried her nose in the silky lining. "God, he smells good." She tossed the jacket aside, then raced back into the living room.

By the time she got there, Liam had the new lamp working. In all honesty, it was a much nicer lamp than the one she'd broken over his head. "It looks great," Ellie said. She twisted her fingers together in front of her, suddenly forgetting what came next. "Drinks!" she said. "Would you like something to drink? I have wine and beer and orange juice. Diet cola and club soda and—"

"Beer would be great," Liam said.

"Good. Why don't you just sit down and I'll get it?" When Ellie reached the kitchen, she opened the refrigerator and stuck her face inside, grateful for the cool air that counteracted the warm blush on her cheeks. She found a bottle of beer and then rummaged through a drawer for a bottle opener.

"Something smells good."

His voice in the kitchen doorway caught her off guard just as she was opening the beer and she jumped. The beer bottle skidded sideways, then spun around twice before rolling off the edge of the counter. Luckily, it hit the small rug in front of the sink. Rather than shattering, it just spewed foam all over her shoes.

In a few long strides he was at her side. He bent and grabbed the beer bottle, then rose just as she leaned over to wipe up the mess with a dish towel. Her chin hit his head, causing her to bite her tongue and Ellie cried out in pain.

Liam took the towel from her, ran a corner under cold water, then handed it back to her. "Here, press this on your tongue."

She did as she was told, now completely mortified by her behavior. He must think she was some kind of loon! "'Anks," Ellie said.

"I guess you haven't really recovered from the other night," Liam commented.

She frowned. "'Aht? 'Ay 'ould 'oo 'ay 'at?"

"Why would I say that? Because you're just a little skittish. I figured you might still be shaken up over everything that happened. Either that, or I make you nervous. Do I make you nervous?"

Ellie took the towel out of her mouth and shook her

head. "No." It was a lie. Just about the biggest lie she'd ever told in her life. "I—I'm just not used to having guests. You're the first person I've met in Boston and I just wanted to make things nice."

"You don't have to try so hard," Liam said, reaching out to take the towel from her hand. He wove his fingers through hers, lifted her hand up to his mouth and gave it a soft kiss. "Just relax."

Ellie stared at the spot where his lips had touched, her breath slowly leaving her lungs. So much for platonic intentions, she mused. Maybe if she tipped the refrigerator on top of herself, he'd kiss her on the mouth.

"Is there another beer in the fridge?" Liam asked.

"Yes," she said, her voice cracking slightly. "I'll get it."

"*I'll* get it," Liam said.

Ellie decided to busy herself at the stove, checking the pasta sauce that was warming on one burner, then salting the water that had come to a boil on the other. "I hope you like pasta."

"I'll eat pretty much anything, especially if it's home cooked. Sean and I eat a lot of take-out and frozen pizza. And we eat at my dad's pub whenever we're working there. I can't remember the last time I had a home-cooked meal."

"Is Sean your roommate?" Ellie asked, anxious to keep the conversation rolling.

Liam took a sip of his beer. "My roommate and brother. We have a place over in Southie, near where we grew up. My dad owns a pub and my brothers and I work there whenever we can."

"You have more than one brother?"

He nodded. "Conor, Dylan, Brendan, Brian, Sean and me. And we have a sister, Keely."

"You're the youngest?"

"Of the boys. Keely's the youngest of all. Where is your family?"

Ellie sighed. "I don't have any family, except for my mother. But I don't know where she is. She took off when I was three or four. I never knew my father. My grandparents raised me and they died while I was in college. So it's just me."

"Sounds like you had a pretty tough childhood," Liam commented.

"No, it was really wonderful. My grandmother was a librarian in this little town in upstate New York. And when I wasn't in school, I hung out at the library with her. I just loved books—I still do. I mean, there's an answer to every question in a book somewhere. You just have to find the right book." She paused, realizing how silly and naive her words sounded.

"What do you do for a living?" Liam asked.

She grabbed up a handful of dried pasta and dropped it into the water, then stirred it with a plastic spoon. "Nothing right now. I'm looking for a new job. I just moved to Boston from Manhattan."

"And what did you do there?"

"I worked in a bank. I'm an accountant."

"Why Boston?"

"I had to get away from New York. I just couldn't work there anymore."

"Why is that?"

Ellie really didn't want to get into a conversation

about all her man troubles, especially with a man she was trying so hard to impress. "I really don't want to talk about that. It's in the past. I'm starting a new life here." She paused, searching for another topic. "I didn't think you wanted to accept my dinner invitation. I thought maybe I was being too bold."

"I don't mind that."

"Some men do. That's always been a bit of a problem with me. I've never really been myself around the men I date—not that I'm dating you. I guess I feel as if I can talk to you. You saved my life."

"Speaking of which, I noticed that you don't have a decent dead bolt on your door. And you could probably use some sash locks on these windows that open onto the back porch. If you'd like, I can pick up some stuff at the hardware store."

Ellie nodded, warmed by his offer. How had a man like Liam Quinn ever stayed single for so long? A sudden thought hit her. What if he wasn't single? What if he had a steady girlfriend? But then surely he wouldn't have accepted her dinner invitation. But what if he'd felt obligated to accept?

"He probably was just looking for money," Liam continued. "You don't keep any large sums of money in the house, do you?"

"No," Ellie said. "I don't have any large sums of money. Why don't we have our salad now while the pasta cooks?" She turned to retrieve the plates from the refrigerator, then walked out of the kitchen into the dining alcove. She set the plates down and Liam held out her chair for her, pushing it in as she sat. Then he took a spot across from her.

He grabbed up the wine she'd put on the table and poured her a glass. "I think we should have a toast," he said. "To the burglar who brought us together."

"And to the white knight who rode to my rescue," Ellie added with a laugh.

Liam's expression shifted slightly and, for a moment, Ellie thought she'd said something terribly wrong. But then he smiled and clinked his beer bottle against her wineglass.

Ellie took a gulp of her wine, watching him over the rim of the goblet. The liquid burned as it went down, but the sensation caused warmth to flood through her limbs, making her relax just a bit. Ellie knew that she'd have to stop after one glass, though. She was having a hard enough time keeping her distance as it was, especially while operating under the influence of Liam Quinn.

3

"WOULD YOU LIKE another glass of wine?" Liam picked up the bottle and filled Ellie's glass, not waiting for a reply. God, she was pretty when she was drunk. Her face was flushed and her eyes glittered with amusement and she kept leaning over the table, giving him a tempting view of her breasts beneath the low-cut neckline of her sweater.

"I really shouldn't," she said with a giggle. "Two glasses is my limit."

Liam didn't have the heart to tell her that she'd reached her limit about three hours ago. The bottle was empty and Ellie Thorpe would probably wake up tomorrow morning with a raging hangover.

Usually, Liam was loath to take advantage of a woman who'd had too much to drink. But his mind wasn't on sex tonight—not that he hadn't thought about pulling Ellie to her feet and dragging her into the bedroom. There was something highly attractive about a woman who was completely unaware of her sexuality.

The way she smiled, the way she reached out and touched him every so often, the way she licked her lips after she took a sip of wine—all of it was driving him a little crazy. But Ellie was guileless, completely unaware of the effect she was having on him.

Liam watched as she stuck her finger into the frosting of the chocolate cake she'd served for dessert, then put her finger in her mouth. He couldn't help but imagine what that mouth might do to him, how her lips might move over his body, how her tongue might taste. He swallowed hard. Maybe this would take more strength than he possessed. He knew enough about women to know that he could have Ellie tonight if he simply asked.

But Liam had to settle a few things before he took that step—if ever. Now that he had her good and drunk, he needed to get her talking. About her job at the bank. About Ronald Pettibone. And about the two hundred and fifty thousand that Sean suspected she'd stolen.

"So, tell me about your job in New York. Why would you leave an exciting city like that to come to Boston?" The question sounded innocuous enough, Liam thought.

"Oh, let's not talk about New York!" Ellie replied. "Bad memories of a very bad man. Make that four or five bad men—I've lost count."

"What about that guy on the sidewalk this morning?" Liam asked, unable to contain his curiosity. There had been something between them, something that hinted at a prior relationship. The more he'd thought about it, the more he'd wondered who the guy had been. He'd gotten a fairly decent look at him, but he didn't resemble the photo of Pettibone. "Was he a bad man?"

Ellie groaned. "He was—or is—nobody." Her

frown quickly turned to a devilish smile. "Are the men better here in Boston? Please tell me they are."

"I don't know. Maybe you should tell me a little more about the men in New York."

"Who do you want to know about? If I tell you, will you promise to drive to New York and beat them all up?"

Liam chuckled. "I'll consider it. Why don't you tell me about the man who made you decide to leave?"

"That was Ronald," she said, crinkling her nose. "Ronald Pettibone. And, let me tell you, he didn't have one petty bone in his body, he had about five hundred. God, I don't know why I always pick the jerks—present company excluded."

"What did Ron—"

"Ronald," Ellie corrected.

"What did Ronald do?"

"He made me fall in love with him. And then he made me into something I never wanted to be. And then he dumped me. And then he had the nerve to ask me to return all the gifts he'd given me."

Liam gazed across the table at her stricken expression. She sure didn't look like a coldhearted criminal. But she did look like a woman who might do anything for love. And sometimes that kind of woman was more dangerous than a woman bent on a life of crime. "Any man who dumps you has got to be a little crazy."

She smiled brightly, reached over and squeezed his hand. "That's a nice thing to say. You're a very nice guy. Have you ever been dumped?"

"A few times," Liam lied.

"I have this really good book you should read." She pushed out of her chair and turned toward the bookcase on the far wall. But the combination of the wine and the quick move caused her knees to buckle. Liam bolted out of his chair and caught her before she hit the floor.

"I think maybe we can leave the book for another time," he murmured, pulling her against his body, his mouth just inches from hers. He could feel the warmth of her breath against his chin and he fought the impulse to capture her lips.

Ellie's eyes fluttered shut and her head swayed from side to side. "Are we dancing?" She wrapped her arms around his neck and sighed. "Let's dance."

"Let's not. I think we better get you to bed."

"Okay. I'm a little drunk, though. I may not remember everything in the morning—but I know it will be good."

"There won't be anything to remember." Liam bent and scooped her into his arms. She rested her head on his shoulder as he carried her into her bedroom.

He set her gently on the bed. Ellie sighed softly, then curled into a little ball, her face pressed into his jacket. "You smell good," she said.

Liam tugged his jacket from beneath her head and slipped it on. He then pulled her shoes off and drew the blanket up around her. As he smoothed a strand of hair from her face, he bent closer and brushed a kiss across her wine-stained lips. "Good night, princess. I'll be watching out for you." With that, Liam turned and walked to the door.

The street was dark and empty when he reached the

sidewalk. He glanced both ways before crossing to his home away from home. Spending the night in Ellie's bed would have been far more comfortable...and convenient. But Liam never seduced a woman who didn't want to be seduced. And, right now, Ellie was in no condition to know what she really wanted.

Though he hadn't gotten the answers he'd been looking for, he'd gotten more. He'd learned enough to know that Ellie Thorpe was incapable of deception or cunning or greed. She was a sweet, beautiful woman, a romantic with a silly streak, a sexy temptress with a little-girl laugh. And Liam knew that the kiss he'd given her wouldn't be the last.

He took the steps up to the attic two at a time, pushed the door open and squinted into the dark, waiting for his eyes to adjust.

"I know where you've been."

Liam jumped at the sound of the voice coming out of the darkness. He spun around to find Sean sitting on the old sofa, his legs stretched out in front of him, his hands locked behind his head.

"Jeez, you scared me!" Liam cried.

His brother pushed to his feet and strolled across the room to the window. He peered through the lens of Liam's camera. "You weren't here. I figured I'd do some surveillance. I saw a man in Eleanor Thorpe's apartment and I thought Pettibone had arrived."

Liam bit back a curse. "Did you snap some pictures?" he asked matter-of-factly.

"I did. But the guy in the apartment was you."

Liam waited for Sean to rip him a new one, but the expected rant didn't come. "All right, I made a mistake. But I was just taking advantage of an opportunity. This is mostly your fault."

"My fault?"

"I'm not a P.I.," Liam said. He grabbed a bottle of water from the cooler and twisted it open. "You can't expect me to know all the rules. A few nights ago some guy broke into her apartment while I was watching her."

"Did you get his photo?"

"No! I ran over to her place and caught the guy before he got to her. She thought I was the intruder and she hit me over the head, tied me up and called the police."

"The police know about this?" This time Sean strung together a colorful variety of curse words.

"They don't know about the stakeout," Liam told him. "Conor smoothed things over. By the way, he wanted me to remind you about the baptism for Riley."

"Don't change the subject. This doesn't explain what you were doing in her apartment tonight."

"This morning, I stopped by the coffee shop a few blocks over and I ran into her. I guess the police gave her the whole story about how I saved her and how I'm a really good guy, so she asked me out to dinner and I had to accept."

Sean raked his fingers through his hair impatiently. "What the hell were you thinking? You could have said no." He shook his head. "Wait, you're Liam Quinn. You don't say no to women."

"I was thinking it would be a helluva lot easier to watch her from inside her apartment, where there's heat, I might add, than from up here. It's freezing up here and there's nothing to do. I've watched her apartment for three days now and nothing has happened."

"A guy broke in."

"Yeah, but maybe that was just a random crime."

"Maybe it was Pettibone paying a midnight visit. Maybe she was expecting him, did you ever think of that? He won't come back with you there."

Liam held up his hand. "Maybe you should just take over here. I'll get out of the way and you can do whatever it is you do."

Sean thought about the option for a long moment, then shook his head. "Now that your cover is blown, you should keep seeing her."

"You want me to date her?"

"See her. If that means a date, then fine, date her. The first chance you get, search her apartment."

Liam frowned. "Isn't that against the law?"

"Not exactly. If she invites you in and you open a few drawers, there's nothing wrong with that. You're not acting as an agent of the police."

"Conor warned me to stay away from her. He kind of figured I was working on a case for you."

"Good."

"So what is it? Do you want me to continue seeing her or do you want me to stop?"

"I don't know."

"Well, let me know when you do." Liam walked back to the cooler and grabbed a ham sandwich. He'd spent so much time dragging Ellie into dinner conversation that he hadn't had much to eat. He took a bite of the sandwich, then moved to the window. "There was one other contact. When I came out of the coffee shop she was talking to a guy. It seemed like they were arguing, but she denied it. When I asked her who he was, she just brushed me off. I didn't want to push the point."

"Was it Pettibone?"

Liam reached for the photo of Ronald Pettibone and stared at it for a long time. "No...I don't know. Maybe. If it was, then he doesn't look anything like this photo. But then Ellie doesn't look anything like her photo."

"If it's him, he'll be back," Sean said, joining him at the window.

"She leaves her curtains open when she undresses," Liam murmured, his gaze fixed on the apartment across the street.

"Oh, yeah?"

Liam pulled the curtains closed. "Don't be a pervert."

"You haven't been looking?"

"Yes. But it was strictly professional."

"And what did you think?"

"She's got a nice body," Liam commented. "A great body. And whoever took that bank photo of her ought to have his shutter finger amputated. It's those kinds of photographers that make us all look like hacks."

"What else did you find out?"

Liam shrugged. "I don't think she's a criminal."

"She's a woman," Sean said, his expression tight. "A beautiful woman. And you're blinded by her beauty."

"I just met her," Liam said. "I don't get blinded until the fourth or fifth date."

"What did you talk about?"

"Life. Romance. Work. Nothing in particular."

"Introduce her to me. I'll date her. *I'd* get answers."

"Oh, right. You'll charm her with your rapier wit and your bubbling conversation," he said sarcastically. "Besides, we're not dating. I had dinner with her, that's all."

"What's her name?"

Liam frowned. "You know what her name is. Ellie. Eleanor Thorpe."

"You're falling for her. The way you say her name. You smile when you say it. I've seen that before. It always means the same thing."

"I'm getting the hell out of here," Liam said. "You've got your case back now—you can watch her."

"I can't. I've got to follow up on the case from Atlantic City. Husband's heading off on a business trip to Syracuse and I've got to trail him there."

"No way. I'm not spending another day in this attic."

"Then spend as much time as you can with her. You have my permission. Whatever you get, you get." Sean walked to the door, but at the last minute he turned around. He reached into his pocket, withdrew a wad of cash, then tossed it to Liam. "Three thousand," he murmured. "That's half of the retainer they gave me. It's yours. Just don't screw this up."

The door closed behind Sean, but Liam didn't move. Instead he stared down at the wad of cash in his hand. Three thousand dollars. He would have spent time with Ellie for free. But now, with the money in his hands, Liam realized that he wasn't just playing at private investigator for his brother. Sean expected him to come through and ultimately that meant putting Ellie Thorpe in jail.

Liam shoved the cash into his pocket. Until this moment the women in his life had been conquests and challenges and, sometimes, lovers. Charming them had been part of his nature. But now, Ellie Thorpe was something else. Charming her was a job—a job he'd been paid to do. And if he was to succeed, he'd have to ignore the urge to romance her.

Liam had never done that before. "I guess there's always a first time," he murmured.

ELLIE STARED at the keypad mounted next to her apartment door. "I thought you were going to buy me a new lock."

Liam smiled and casually draped his arm over her shoulder. "You remember that conversation?"

She felt a blush warm her cheeks at the memory of their dinner. And the blush was intensified by the blood pounding through her veins at his touch. Ellie knew it was simply a friendly gesture, but the warmth of his arm against her nape made her knees a little weak and her brain a little fuzzy.

She couldn't deny her attraction to him. What woman wouldn't be attracted? That dark hair that never seemed to see a comb. And those eyes, always with a devilish twinkle that made him seem all the more dangerous. Ellie knew she couldn't let herself surrender to that kind of charm, but sometimes she couldn't help herself. "I remember most of what happened," Ellie murmured. "Especially the headache I had the next morning."

Though she'd been more than a little tipsy, the wine hadn't affected her memory, just her inhibitions. The things she'd said to him, the things she'd done, still brought a flood of embarrassment. She remembered throwing her arms around his neck and begging him to dance. She also remembered being scooped up into his arms and carried to the bedroom. And she remembered how much she'd wanted him to kiss her. But after that her memory got very fuzzy.

Still, it didn't matter. Memory or none, when she woke up fully dressed the next morning, Ellie knew that nothing had happened. Liam Quinn had been the perfect gentleman. Maybe it was all for the best, Ellie mused. If something were to happen between her and Liam, she'd certainly want to be in full possession of her faculties when it did.

"I'm never going to drink wine again. And I'm never going to figure out how to use this. Look at all these buttons and lights."

"This is better than a new lock," Liam said, handing her the manual. "It's a whole security system. It will keep burglars out."

Ellie groaned inwardly as she took the manual from his fingers and wandered over to the sofa. Every time she had to program her VCR, she had to spend a half hour with the manual. She'd even found a self-help book called *Electronics Anxiety*, written specifically for people who were frightened of their computers and VCRs and alarm clocks. But it hadn't helped.

And now she'd be held prisoner in her apartment by

a bunch of wires and circuits and a very loud alarm. She wasn't sure she'd ever want to go out again. "But I don't need a security system. I could just get a dog."

A very loud dog. But then she'd have to feed it and walk it. Ellie sighed inwardly. A man would be a better choice. If she had a man in her bed every night, she'd be able to get some sleep...or maybe not. Especially if she had a man like Liam Quinn in her bed. "Stop it," she murmured, pinching her eyes shut and driving the thoughts from her mind once again. "How much is this going to cost? I can't afford this now."

Liam glanced over at the security technician who was picking up the last of his tools. "Ed is a friend of my brother, Conor. He put the system in at the pub. He's doing this one as a favor."

"All right," Ed said. "These are the keys for the new locks. All the directions for programming in the code are in the manual. It's easier than programming a VCR. I've wired all the windows and the door, so if any of them is opened when the alarm is set, it will go off. I've also installed glass-break sensors. The alarm will go to the security company who will call the police."

"Great. Thanks, Ed."

"Yeah, thanks, Ed," Ellie echoed.

"No problem," he said. "Call me and we'll set up a time for you to come over and take pictures." After Liam shut the door behind Ed, he turned to Ellie and smiled.

"Pictures?" she asked.

"He wants some photos of him riding around town on his new motorcycle. I told him I'd take some."

"Then this wasn't really free."

"It was a good trade. And now you're safe."

"No," Ellie countered, "my stuff is safe. No one can get in when I'm not here."

"And no one can get in when you *are* here. Or if they do, the alarm will go off and the police will come. Believe me, when that horn goes off, the burglar isn't going to stick around."

"I'm not sure I'm going to be able to work this."

"Come here," he said. "I'll show you how. It's easy." Reluctantly, Ellie got off the sofa and crossed the room to the door. "You just push the star key twice, then wait for the red light, then punch in your code. We'll do 3-5-5-4. See, that spells 'E-L-L-I.' Ellie. That turns it on and shuts it off. I'll make an extra copy of your new keys to leave with the security company. If the alarm goes off when you're out, they'll come over and check the apartment."

"I guess," Ellie said. "But this whole thing scares me."

"It's meant to keep you safe," Liam replied.

"Safe from what? Do you think that burglar will be back?"

"Probably not. But it's better safe than sorry."

"You're right," Ellie said. She stared at the keypad, a tiny sliver of fear niggling at her brain. What if the burglar did come back and Liam wasn't here to save her? The burglar obviously hadn't gotten what he'd come for.

Liam's finger hooked beneath her chin and he lifted her gaze up to his. "You don't have to be afraid, Ellie."

"I know. Thank you."

Liam leaned closer and touched his lips to hers in the gentlest of kisses. He kissed her as if it had been the most natural thing in the world, as if he hadn't even thought about it before acting on the impulse.

"Feel better?"

"Not really. Can you do it again?" It was only after the words left her mouth that she realized what she'd said. He'd wanted to know if she felt better about the security system not if the kiss made her feel better.

"I'll try," Liam said. He slipped his hands around her waist and pulled her toward him. The instant his lips touched hers, Ellie's limbs went weak, her heart fluttered in her chest and she thought she might just hyperventilate.

It was clear from the way he brought his mouth down on hers that Liam Quinn was a very accomplished kisser. She tried not to think about all the women he must have kissed to get so good at it, yet she had to give credit for what they'd contributed to his rather formidable talent.

His tongue slipped along the crease of her lips and Ellie took it as an invitation to open her mouth. When she did, he deepened the kiss, and suddenly she realized just how unprepared for this she was. Desire snaked through her body, coiling in the pit of her stomach. This was need like she'd never felt it before, a deep physical ache that only seemed to be exacerbated by his taste and his touch.

Ellie smoothed her hands over his broad chest, her fingers searching the contours of flesh and bone. He was perfect, more perfect than she deserved, and Ellie wondered at the luck that had brought him running into her apartment that night. She wasn't about to question it, and instead decided to revel in it. A girl like her usually didn't get a chance with a guy like Liam.

He slowly pulled away, stealing one last kiss before he spoke. "I have to go," he murmured.

Ellie's heart sank. She'd imagined that she could continue kissing him for the rest of the afternoon and well into the night.

"I have to go photograph a rally outside Faneuil Hall," he continued, brushing his lips over hers. "It has something to do with...sweatshop labor in...Third World countries."

"That's a serious problem," Ellie murmured, pushing up on her toes and kissing him again.

"The *Globe* called this morning. It's a nice assignment." His lips found the curve of her neck and lingered there for a moment.

"I have to type up a few more letters and send out some résumés," Ellie said. "And I'm going over to the library to get online. I thought I'd post my résumé with a few of the sites on the Web."

"How's the job hunt going?" Liam asked.

"Not great. I've hit all the major banks in Boston and now I'm going to have to start on the minor ones. I've had four years in banking but maybe I should consider a change. I could get my C.P.A. and work for an accounting firm. Or maybe find a position with a small business."

"You'll find something," Liam said, reaching out to smooth his hand along her cheek. "You're smart and you're capable and you're awfully pretty to look at."

"And if you kiss me again, I promise to believe that," Ellie murmured.

He did as he was told, then grabbed his jacket and bid her goodbye, promising to call her later that evening. Ellie closed the door behind him and smiled. She touched her lips, still damp from his kiss, then tried to remember exactly how wonderful it felt. Later on, she could summon that memory and relish it all over again.

It felt good to be kissed again. And touched and held. Though she'd tried so hard to resist him, Ellie had known going in that she'd once again be putting her heart at risk. And now that feeling was even more acute. She was falling hard and fast for Liam Quinn and she couldn't seem to stop herself.

She couldn't pinpoint exactly what it was that made him so irresistible, but he had a certain charm that she found incredibly attractive. He always knew just the right thing to say, yet he never tried too hard. There were moments when she felt as if he was madly in love with her and then other times when he'd pull away and keep her guessing. It was like a little dance between them, each advancing and retreating at different times, trying to read the subtleties in every word and action.

She'd come to Boston to get away from her rather disastrous history with men. And then, against all odds, she'd stumbled across the man who very well could be the man of her dreams. Ellie hurried over to her bookshelf and ran her fingers along the rows of books until she found what she wanted. *"Find the Man of Your Dreams,*" she said, pulling out a volume she'd purchased three years ago.

She settled down on the sofa, tucking her feet up underneath her. Now that she'd found him, Ellie would have to figure out how to keep him. Maybe the book would have some good advice.

THE IMAGE appeared slowly, the grays intensifying as Liam swirled the photo around in the developer. This was the best part of photography, he mused. That moment of anticipation, waiting to see what the camera had captured.

He'd shut himself in the darkroom that occupied the spare bedroom in the apartment, ready to catch up on some film he'd taken a few weeks before. After all, there wasn't much he could do once Ellie went to sleep. She was safe inside her apartment, the security system set to warn her of any intruders. But instead of grabbing the film he'd taken of children playing on Boston Common, he'd grabbed the roll he'd taken that first night in the attic.

An outline of a figure appeared first on the photo paper and then more and more detail. "Come on, sweetheart," he murmured. "Show yourself." He'd taken the photo that first night and until now hadn't thought about developing it. But after a week of Ellie, the curiosity had been too much to resist.

He pulled the photo out of the developer and slipped it into the stop bath, then sat on a stool and stared at the image. Lord, she was beautiful. He'd caught her in a moment when she'd been completely vulnerable, her hair tousled around her face, her incredible body draped in a silk robe, the fabric falling over delicious curves, her head turned slightly to the side.

His gaze focused on her mouth as he moved the photo to the fixer fluid. The memory of their kiss flooded his brain, the feel of her lips beneath his, and the taste of her, warm and sweet. Need snaked through his body, from his brain to his gut, and Liam groaned softly. Hell, he hadn't wanted to kiss her. In truth, he'd been fighting it for all he was worth. But Liam had never been a guy to ignore his instincts and Ellie's mouth had been just too tempting to resist.

He tried to rationalize his attraction to her and the only thing he could come up with was that she was forbidden fruit. The fact that he shouldn't want her made her even more impossible to resist. And then there was that photo Sean had shown him, the prim and proper banker. He'd seen the other side and Liam suspected that there was a very passionate woman hidden beneath the accountant exterior.

"This has got to stop," Liam muttered, rubbing a knot of tension from the back of his neck. Ellie Thorpe was a dangerous woman to want. Besides, this was just a job. And the kiss they'd shared had been part of the job, a ploy to get her to trust him and to confide in him.

A knock sounded on the door of the darkroom. His brother wasn't supposed to be home for another day or two. "Sean?" he called.

"It's Brian. I'm looking for Sean."

Liam sighed and dropped the photo in the water bath. "He's out of town. Hartford, I think. On a case."

"Can I come in?"

"Yeah," Liam called. "It's all right."

Liam pulled the door open. As always, Brian was immaculately dressed. A well-tailored wardrobe had become part of his rising profile in Boston. Brian was the most popular investigative reporter at WBTN-TV. His face was plastered on billboards all around town and he could be seen every few nights on the eleven o'clock news, reporting on some scandal about to rock the city. Right now, with his tie draped around his neck and his collar unbuttoned, he'd obviously finished with work for the night.

"Jeez, you look like hell," Brian commented.

"Thanks. Coming from a guy like you, I'll take that as a compliment."

Brian stepped into the glow of the red safelight that illuminated the darkroom. He looked around, like the reporter he was, always searching for something to pique his interest. "What do you need?" Liam asked.

Brian shrugged, the shoulders of his tailored suit rising then falling. "I'm working on a story. I needed Sean to track someone down for me."

"He's busy with a divorce case. I'm picking up the slack for him."

"What are you working on?" Brian asked.

Liam glanced down at the photo of Ellie still swirling in the water. Brian followed his gaze. "Who is she?"

"No one."

"She's awfully pretty for no one. Let me guess. She's too pretty to be the unhappy wife, so she must be the other woman."

"Yeah, she is," Liam lied. He pulled the photo out of

the water and hung it on the line. "What are you doing out so late? It's nearly one."

"I've been working on a story. I find that people are much more likely to talk if I catch them after a long night of drinking. So I just follow my sources from bar to bar."

Brian sat on a stool and slowly began to flip through a pile of Liam's photos. He picked up one of a homeless man. "This is nice. Sometimes I work so hard to get a good piece of tape, a great sound bite, an interesting reaction. But it never seems as powerful as a single moment captured in a photo. This is real. It has impact."

"What has you waxing philosophical?" Liam asked. "Let me guess. A woman?"

"I wish," Brian said.

"The only other thing it could be is your career. I've been seeing your face on every bus in Boston. The career must be going well."

"Nah. It's not exactly going the way I planned. They want to put me behind the anchor desk. I've got a great Q-rating, men trust me, women like to look at me. I can do big things for the station. At least, that's what they're telling me."

"What's wrong with that?"

"I wouldn't be reporting news," Brian said, his voice passionate. "I'd be reading it. I've been thinking about quitting, maybe trying print journalism. My face won't make a difference at a newspaper. Or I could freelance. There are a lot of magazines that publish investigative pieces."

Brian had always been completely fixated when it

came to work. "Come on, Brian. You have a regular job that pays well. Everyone in town knows you. You get great women, classy women, and you want to give it all up? Give me a break."

"When you put it that way, it does sound a little screwy," Brian murmured.

Liam strode out of the darkroom and Brian followed him. Though his brother obviously wanted to discuss his problems in greater detail, Liam really wasn't in the mood. He had enough troubles of his own. Unlike Brian, Liam never knew when his next paycheck would arrive. No one in town was interested in his photos. And the one woman he found attractive was probably a felon.

"I gotta go," Liam murmured.

"You going over to the pub?"

"No, I've got somewhere else I have to be," Liam replied.

"When is Sean getting back?" Brian called.

"I don't know. I'm not his secretary. Sean has his cell phone with him. The number is on the refrigerator. Just lock up before you leave."

Liam closed the door behind him and jogged down the steps, heading for his car. He wasn't sure where he was going. He'd just drive, hoping to clear his head. He started the car and pulled away from the curve, heading into Boston. But when his thoughts kept returning to Ellie Thorpe, he opened the window and let the chill and damp of the early April night roar through the car. He drove out of South Boston and crossed the bridge into Chinatown, then at the last moment turned onto Atlantic Avenue, choosing a route along the Boston waterfront.

It wasn't until he got to the Charlestown Bridge that Liam realized where he was headed. The bridge led right into the tangle of one-way streets in Charlestown. He made the circle on Main Street, determined to head over to Cambridge. But, in the end, Liam headed in the direction of Ellie's apartment.

He pulled up across the street from her apartment building and parked the car. Leaning against the back of the seat, he stared up at the dark windows of her apartment, trying to imagine her inside, curled up in her bed, her dark hair spread across the pillow.

His hands clenched instinctively as he remembered the silken feel of her hair between his fingers. With a low curse, he shoved open the car door and stepped out. Liam paced the length of his car a few times, unwilling to climb the stairs to the attic simply to look through his lens at a dark apartment.

"Jeez, and I thought Brian was screwed up," he muttered. He got back inside the car and started it, dragging in a deep breath as he put it into gear. Maybe Brian had the right idea. Quinn's Pub would be open for at least another hour. Liam could do a lot of damage in that amount of time.

If a few pints of Guinness didn't get rid of this preoccupation with Ellie Thorpe, then he'd have a few more.

4

LIAM STARED out the front windshield of his car, the view of the Charlestown neighborhood blurred by the drizzling rain. "I want out," he murmured. "I don't care about the money. Consider the work I've put in so far my gift to you."

"You can't," Sean replied. "We're too close. Sooner or later Pettibone has got to show up."

"How do you know he hasn't got the money?" Liam asked. "How do you know that he didn't pull this off on his own?"

"You said it yourself. They were lovers. She admitted that much to you. Pettibone took that money and she has to be in on it. They're playing it cool. Staying away from each other so they don't arouse suspicion."

"I don't like this," Liam said. "She seems like a nice person."

"Some criminals are nice," Sean said. "Embezzlers win over your trust, then they rob you blind. It's part of the M.O."

"Wouldn't it be easier just to confront her? I could just ask her if she stole the money and watch her reaction. I read people pretty well and I'll know if she's lying."

"And then what? She's going to hand it over?" Sean laughed. "That's a plan."

"Maybe. Maybe she could make a deal and give the money back in exchange for them dropping all charges."

"Li, what is your problem with this woman?"

"I don't have a problem."

"Then just do the damn job," Sean said. "It's your watch, I'm going home." He opened the car door and stepped out into the rain. At the last moment Sean braced his arms on the edge of the roof and leaned back inside. "Don't screw this up. We're close. Let's just finish it."

Sean slammed the door and Liam watched him jog to his car. He tipped his head back and sighed. This whole thing had gotten way out of hand. Though he was used to charming women, his main goal had always been a passionate night in bed followed by breakfast the next morning. Both parties were left well satisfied and nobody got hurt.

But this was different. His goal here was to put Ellie Thorpe in jail. And the more time he spent with her, the more he began to feel that no matter what she'd done, she didn't deserve twenty years behind bars.

With a low curse, he raked his hand through his damp hair. After the kiss they'd shared, Liam felt as if he was the one in prison. Thoughts of her filled his head, the way she tasted, the soft warmth of her body in his arms, and his instant and very intense reaction. Kissing women had always been one of the true pleasures in life for him. But with Ellie, it had been different. Kissing her had been exciting and disturbing and confusing all at once.

It hadn't been just one kiss, either. Over the past few

days they'd spent a fair amount of time repeating that first encounter. Every moment they spent together seemed to be filled with tension that only a long and very deep kiss could relieve.

"To hell with this," Liam muttered, shoving open the door. As he'd told Sean, all he had to do was ask and he'd have his answer. But as he walked toward Ellie's apartment, he realized that after he had his answer, the questions would only become more complicated. Right now Ellie was a beautiful woman, bright, sexy, funny. He'd known his fair share of women and they all possessed similar qualities, but Ellie had them in a unique combination.

But what was it that made her different? Was it the secrets she kept? Had Liam found her attractive because, for once in his life, he couldn't read a woman's thoughts? There were moments when he wished he could strip away everything, like peeling away layers of clothes. The closer they got to intimacy, the closer he got to the truth.

Liam glanced over his shoulder as he crossed the street to her apartment. If he crossed that bridge, he might never come back. It was clear from the intensity of the kisses they'd shared that he and Ellie would be incredible together. Even now he could imagine the feel of her skin beneath his hands, the weight of her body on top of his, and the heat that would race through his blood when he was inside her. If he tasted that, there might be no going back.

He pulled his cell phone out of his pocket and dialed her number, then stared up at the third-floor windows. When she answered, he caught himself grinning. "Hey, there."

"Hi," Ellie said.

Liam imagined her face, the tiny smile curling her lips, her eyes bright. "What are you doing?"

"Working on cover letters, reading the want ads. I made a few calls to some headhunters about jobs in Washington, D.C., and Chicago."

Liam's jaw went tight at her comment. He didn't want to think that she'd be walking out of his life as quickly as she'd walked in. "Why don't you forget about that and come out with me?"

"Where are we going?" Ellie asked.

"I don't know. I thought, since you're new to the city, I'd show you the sights of Boston. I'll pick you up in ten or fifteen seconds. Be ready."

He switched the phone off, then took the front steps to her building two at a time. When he'd buzzed her apartment, she'd unlocked her door and was waiting for him on the third-floor landing. She wore a faded pair of jeans and a bulky wool sweater. Her dark hair was tied back in a pretty scarf, and though she wore very little makeup, she still managed to look gorgeous.

"Where were you?" Ellie asked.

"Out front," Liam said, jogging up the stairs. Without even thinking, he grabbed her around the waist and gave her a quick kiss, their tongues touching for an instant and the taste of her going straight to his head.

"You're a pretty confident guy, aren't you?" she murmured, pressing her palms against his chest.

"No one can resist my charm," Liam teased. "Get your jacket. It's raining."

She disappeared inside the apartment, but Liam decided to stay in the hall. The urge to spend the afternoon necking on her sofa would be too much to resist. When she reappeared, she'd pulled a rain hat over her head and bundled herself in a jacket. She handed him her umbrella as she zipped up her jacket.

"We won't need the umbrella," he said.

"Let's walk. I want to go see that pointy thing and it's a perfect day for a walk."

"It's raining," Liam said.

"I was reading this book last night called *Experience Your Life*. It was all about living for the moment. A walk in the rain can be refreshing."

"It's wet," Liam said.

"It can cleanse the soul. Everyone needs their soul cleansed now and then."

"All right," Liam said, figuring his soul could use a decent bath. "We'll go to the pointy thing, which just happens to be the very famous Bunker Hill monument."

"That's even better. We'll get some history with our walk."

Liam grabbed her hand and tucked it in the crook of his arm as they started in the direction of Monument Square, a place he'd visited countless times as a Boston schoolboy. But they'd just reached the other side of the street when he remembered his camera. The light was unusual, the sun filtering through the haze every now and then, and the rain shimmered off the pavement, exactly the kinds of conditions for a great photo. "Wait here," he said. "I'm going to run back to get my camera."

He turned and jogged to his car, then retrieved one of his older cameras from the bag in the trunk. It was loaded with black and white film, but he grabbed a roll of color just in case. Liam hung the camera around his neck and strode down the sidewalk. When he reached the intersection, he stepped off the curb, intending to walk back to where he'd left Ellie.

She waved and called to him and he paused, thinking what a pretty picture she made in her rain slicker. She started across the street toward him and he lifted his camera, catching her through the lens.

Liam wasn't sure what made him look away. Probably the sound of a car engine racing and the whir of tires on wet pavement. He caught a blur of movement out of the corner of his eye and shouted to Ellie to stop. As if the entire world slowed, Liam watched the confused expression on her face. She glanced to her left and saw the black sedan racing toward her.

Startled, she froze for a moment and Liam's heart stopped when he realized that she was about to be hit and he could never get to her in time to push her out of the way. But Ellie's reflexes were quicker than he expected and she spun and threw herself at the front bumper of the car parked behind her. She fell to the wet pavement and the car roared away, splashing up a wave of dirty water that sprayed over her.

Once Liam saw that she was all right, he turned the camera in the direction of the car and quickly snapped off a few shots of the rear license plate. Although Ellie had stepped into the intersection unexpectedly, Liam got the distinct feeling that the car had been aiming for her.

When he reached her, Ellie was just struggling to her feet, her face dripping with gray water and the knees of her jeans muddy and scraped. He gently took her arm and tucked her into his embrace, skimming his hand along her body to see if she was still in one piece. "Are you all right?"

"I didn't see him coming," Ellie said in a shaky voice. "I looked but then he just came out of nowhere. If you hadn't called to me, he would have hit me." She pressed her hands against his chest and stared up at him. "You saved my life...again."

Liam furrowed his hand through her damp hair and pulled her close, pressing a kiss to her forehead. Though he'd had his doubts about his part in "saving her life" that first time around, he knew he couldn't deny his part this time. She was right. If he hadn't heard the car, she'd probably be lying in the middle of the street right now, seriously injured...or worse.

"Let's go get you cleaned up," he murmured, his lips pressed against her temple. His heart still slammed in his chest and he consciously willed it to slow, worried that she might sense his panic. If the driver had actually been out to hit her, then Liam was going to find out why.

He slipped his arm around her shoulders and then crossed back to the sidewalk that ran in front of her building. But as he walked, Liam had the uneasy sense that the burglar and the car were somehow tied together. And that the case he was working on for Sean was at the bottom of both near-death experiences.

ELLIE PULLED HER KEYS out of her pocket and, with a trembling hand, tried to push the key into the lock. But no matter how hard she tried, it wouldn't go in. For a moment she felt as if she'd pass out, or throw up, or just start weeping uncontrollably. But she couldn't decide which, so she just stood numbly on the front stoop of the building, the keys dangling from her fingers.

"Here," Liam murmured. "Let me." He reached around her and opened the door, then gave her a gentle push inside. They climbed the stairs to her apartment without speaking and when they reached the third floor, he opened that door, too, making sure to deactivate the alarm.

Ellie headed for the sofa, but Liam stopped her and helped her out of her jacket. Then he turned her to face him. "Are you sure you're all right?"

Ellie nodded, giving her hands a shake to keep them from going numb. "Yes. I am. I just need a moment."

Liam smiled down at her and brushed a thumb along her cheek. "Come on. Why don't you get out of those dirty clothes and into something dry? Or maybe you should take a nice hot bath."

"Okay," Ellie said.

He pulled her into his embrace and she laid her head against his chest. She felt as if she could stay in his arms forever, that if she just waited, his touch would banish all of her fears. That car had passed within a few inches of her and she'd never seen it coming. An image of what might have been flashed in her mind and Ellie pinched her eyes shut and tried to put the horrible thoughts aside.

"First, I wasn't safe in my apartment and now I'm not safe outside it, either."

"This wasn't your fault," Liam said, softly stroking her hair. "You and the car were just trying to occupy the same space at the same time."

"I've had a streak of bad luck," she said. "This book I'm reading called *The Secrets of Self-Determination* says that there is no such thing as bad luck. That we create every situation that we find ourselves in. But I don't believe that. There was the burglary. Why did that guy choose my place? The people downstairs have a much nicer television. And I've had a terrible time finding a job. And I didn't make that big brick fall off the roof of my building."

"What brick?" Liam asked.

"It happened a few days ago. I was leaving for an interview and this brick came flying out of the sky and nearly hit me on the head. It looked exactly like one of the bricks from my building so I called the landlord to tell him he had some serious safety issues."

"Was there a problem?"

"No," Ellie said, frowning. "He found a few bricks on the roof but he figured that there were kids playing up there. They sometimes crawl up the back porches." She smiled weakly. "Maybe I should take that bath. That might calm me down."

"Do you want anything?" Liam asked. "I could make you a cup of tea."

"That would be nice," she said.

She wandered into the bathroom and sat on the edge of the old claw-footed tub. But suddenly she felt too exhausted to move. Though she'd only known

Liam for ten days, he'd already become such a presence in her life. If she'd been alone on the street... If he hadn't called out... If he weren't here now to make her feel safe and secure... "My white knight," she murmured, reaching over to turn on the water.

As the tub slowly began to fill, Ellie slipped out of her wet shoes and damp socks. Then she tugged her sweater over her head. The grimy water hadn't reached the cotton camisole she wore underneath, but the damp still had seeped into her bones. Ellie rubbed her forearms as she stared into the tub.

"Here's your tea."

She glanced up at Liam who watched her from the bathroom door. "Thanks."

"I'm not much of a tea drinker so I didn't make it the regular way. I just nuked the water and stuck in a tea bag. I hope it's all right."

She took a sip of the lemony brew and it immediately began to warm her. "It's perfect." Ellie sucked in a deep breath then looked at him, fixing her gaze on his. "Can I ask you something?"

"Sure."

"Do you think that car was trying to hit me?"

An uneasy look flitted across Liam's handsome face before he hid it behind a warm smile. "Why would someone want to run you over?"

"I—I don't know. I'm just—" Ellie waved her hand, then set the mug down beside the tub. She stood and nervously refolded a bath towel and hung it on the rack.

Liam came up behind her and placed his hands on her shoulders. Ellie tipped her head back and sighed as he softly massaged the tension from her neck. His touch felt so good, strong and sure. She moaned softly and focused on the warmth of his fingers as they skimmed across her shoulders and back. But when he pushed aside the strap of her camisole and pressed his mouth to her shoulder, she froze, her breath caught in her throat.

Then, as if all the fear had been suddenly washed away, Ellie turned to face him. She stared up into his eyes, with their indescribable mix of gold and green. Her gaze drifted down to his mouth and she remembered every kiss they'd shared, how exciting and exhilarating it had all been. She wanted that again, something sweet and soft to occupy her thoughts.

Ellie pushed up on her toes and touched her lips to his. But a brief kiss wasn't enough and she decided she wanted more. Hesitantly she wrapped her arms around his neck and pulled him toward her, her mouth meeting his with a clumsy bump.

But Liam didn't seem to mind. He pulled her against his chest and gently explored her mouth with his tongue, teasing and tasting, lingering over her lips. Ellie knew she shouldn't let it go any further. They barely knew each other. But in the past days, she'd learned to trust Liam with her life. How could a man who'd saved her not once but twice possibly turn around and hurt her?

His hands slipped beneath her camisole and spanned her waist as he deepened the kiss. She'd wanted the taste of him to drive all the worry out of her head, but it was also sweeping her common sense right along with it. She'd made a vow to stay away from men for at least a year. She'd kept that vow for sixty-seven days and about six hours, and with just a few incredible kisses she was ready to throw it all aside.

Liam Quinn was not Ronald Pettibone. Nor was he Brian Keller, the stock analyst she'd been with before Ronald. Nor Steve Winston, the business consultant. Or any of the others that she'd thought she'd loved. Liam was...different. He was a man she could depend upon.

"I read this book once that said that people who have near-death experiences sometimes become more passionate in the aftermath. Do you think that's what's happening here?"

"I don't know. Is that a bad thing?"

Ellie shook her head. "I don't think so. It's just the author's observation."

"Maybe we should stop."

She reached for the hem of her camisole and slowly pulled it up. "Maybe we shouldn't." Ellie gazed into his eyes, waiting for a cue, anything that would tell her that he wanted her as much as she wanted him. He slid his hand up along her rib cage and cupped her breast, stroking his thumb across her nipple and bringing it to an aching peak through the soft fabric.

"You are so beautiful," he murmured. "From the moment I first saw you, I thought about this." He pressed his forehead against hers. "You were dancing a—" he paused "—around me with that—that phone in your hand, dressed in your nightgown." He grinned. "You know, when you stood in front of the light, I could see right through it."

"You looked?"

"I couldn't help myself."

She pulled her camisole up a few more inches, until it was bunched beneath her breasts. "I'm lucky I tied you up," she teased. "I didn't realize how dangerous you were."

Liam chuckled softly, then brushed her hands away. "You like dangerous?" He took the soft cotton knit in his hands and slowly dragged it up and over her head. Then he tossed it aside.

This time when his hand touched her breast, the contact was electric, sending a shockwave through her body. "I do like dangerous," Ellie murmured. "Very much."

With a low growl, Liam reached down and grabbed her, pulling her up until she sat on the edge of the bathroom sink. He covered her mouth with a deep and shattering kiss and Ellie had no choice but to respond. He seemed to know exactly what she wanted. Every place he touched and kissed ached in the moments before his lips moved there.

She couldn't deny that she wanted him, but it was a need that was irrational. With every other man, the weeks or even months that approached this moment had been measured carefully, as if following some pre-scribed schedule. But now she didn't care. So what if she'd only known Liam for ten days? So what if he'd probably seduced a string of beautiful women? That didn't matter.

For now all that mattered was that she wanted him. Ellie reached for the buttons on his shirt and fumbled with them until they were undone. Then she brushed aside the soft cotton and smoothed her hands over his chest, lost in the pure masculine beauty of his body.

His chest was broad and finely muscled, a thin line of hair leading from his collarbone to beneath the waistband of his jeans. She trailed her fingers along that line as if it were a map to the next spot in their seduction. When she reached for the button on his jeans, Liam pushed her hands aside.

He worked the zipper on her jeans until they loosened around her waist. Then, lifting her, he pulled them down her hips, skimming her panties along with them. As he set her back on the countertop Ellie didn't care that she was completely naked and he was still fully dressed. Somehow it made the moment seem more wicked. But she really didn't realize how wicked it was about to become.

She expected him to start on his own clothes next, but instead he slowly explored her body with his lips and his tongue. Perched on the edge of the sink, she felt as if she might slip off at any moment and tumble onto the floor. But his hands were on her body, strong and sure.

Liam trailed his tongue from her nipple to her belly and then paused, gently parting her legs. Ellie sucked in a sharp breath as his mouth found its next destination. The pleasure was so intense that if she moved, she was certain she'd dissolve into a puddle on the floor. Her limbs became weightless and she couldn't keep a rational thought in her mind. All she could do was experience the pleasure he gave her.

Ellie ran her fingers through his hair, arching into him with every sensation. She wanted to hold back, afraid to allow such vulnerability in herself. But the ache inside begged to be relieved. Second by second, she came closer, his tongue testing her limits. And then, as if something inside her burst, Ellie cried out.

Spasms of ecstasy rocked her body and she clutched the edge of the sink, certain that if she fell, she'd tumble into oblivion, destroyed by such an incredible orgasm. But Liam brought her down slowly and gently, until she felt completely relaxed and sated.

"Feel better?" he murmured, pressing his mouth against the curve of her neck.

A shiver of desire raced through her. "I guess the book was right," she murmured.

"Are you ready for your bath now? The tub is almost full."

Ellie didn't care about a bath. Right now, she wanted to drag Liam Quinn into her bedroom to continue what he'd started, making wild and crazy love for the rest of the afternoon. But she wasn't sure how to ask for what she wanted and, in the end, simply nodded her head.

"A bath would be nice."

CANDLELIGHT FLICKERED against the walls of Ellie's bathroom and she sighed softly as she sank back into the steaming water, submerging to her chin. Liam watched from the doorway, a glass of wine in his hand.

She looked so beautiful, so relaxed, he was almost tempted to carry her from the tub to her bed and make love to her. But Liam had stopped just short of that for a reason. Though he'd wanted nothing more than to pleasure Ellie, he knew that if he lost himself in the same pleasures, he'd be taking a risk that might prove costly in the end.

Over and over again he'd had to remind himself that he was still working for Sean. He had a job to do, and no matter how intense his feelings ran for Ellie, there was a chance that she'd committed a crime.

But was that really what he was afraid of? In his heart he knew she wasn't capable of such deceit. But she was capable of something much more dangerous. She could steal his heart, make him fall head over heels in love with her. And that was the last thing he wanted to do.

Liam slowly walked to the tub and squatted beside it. "Here," he murmured.

Ellie opened her eyes and turned to look at him. She smiled then took the glass from him. "I guess my tea got cold."

Liam nodded. "The wine will relax you."

"I don't think I need to be any more relaxed," she said. Ellie sat up, the water skimming off her breasts and leaving her skin slick and shiny. She set the glass on the tiled floor, then reached out and ran her fingers through his hair. "I'm fine," she said.

"You're sure?"

Ellie nodded. "It was just an...accident. Nothing more. He didn't see me, I didn't see him. It was stupid. I should have been paying more attention. And from now on, I will."

"Good," Liam said, leaning forward to drop a kiss on her damp lips. "I can't come riding to your rescue all the time."

But Liam knew that he wasn't going to rest until he knew exactly who had been driving that car. The windows had been tinted, but he was pretty sure he'd gotten a decent shot of the license plate. If there was any connection between the driver and Ronald Pettibone, he'd find out—and he'd make Pettibone pay.

"Would you like me to wash your hair?" he asked.

Ellie nodded.

Liam levered to his feet, grabbed the mugful of tea and dumped it in the sink. When he returned to the tub, he reached down and scooped up some water, then carefully poured it over her head. Ellie handed him a bottle of shampoo and, after her hair was drenched, he squeezed a small bit into his hand and massaged it into her hair.

He'd never really indulged in such tasks with a woman. There was an undeniable intimacy found in waiting on her, in the simple act of helping her bathe. In a way, it all seemed more intimate than what they'd shared earlier. That had been about desire and need, but this was about comfort and affection.

The phone rang and Ellie opened her eyes. "Do you want me to get that?" Liam asked.

"No," she said. "Let the machine pick it up."

"All right," Liam murmured. He moved his fingers down to her nape and gently scrubbed. After four rings the answering machine picked up and they listened as her outgoing message echoed through the empty apartment. Then the beep sounded and a male voice replaced hers.

"Hi, Eleanor. It's Ronald. Listen, I was just calling to apologize about the other day. You just took me by surprise. I didn't expect to feel...well, what I wanted to say was that I really need to see you again. Soon. We have to talk. I've got some contacts at a few banks here in town and...well, we'll discuss that when we see each other. I'm at the Bostonian. Room 215. Call me." The answering machine beeped again at the end of the message.

Liam's fingers slowly dropped to her shoulders. Ronald Pettibone? Damn it, when had she seen Ronald Pettibone? He'd been with her almost constantly over the last ten days. And when he hadn't been with her, either he or Sean had been watching her.

"I guess that wasn't about a job," Ellie said with a light laugh. "How embarrassing to have one man call me when I'm in the tub with another."

For a while he'd almost forgotten what had brought him and Ellie together in the first place. And now, sitting in her bathroom, her naked in the tub, he realized what a colossal mess he'd made of it all. Sean had warned him and he'd refused to listen, certain that he had everything under control. But he should have realized from the very moment he'd first seen Ellie that he was in trouble. If not then, their first kiss should have been a big clue. He should never have let it get this far.

He cleared his throat and hoped that his voice would sound indifferent. "Who is Ronald?" Liam already knew the answer to that question, but it was a logical one to ask considering the circumstances.

"You remember. I told you about him. He's a co-worker from New York," Ellie explained. "Well, more than a co-worker. Not anymore but—" She twisted around until she could look into his eyes. "We used to be…an item."

"Is that another way of saying you used to be lovers?"

"Yes. But nobody knew. We kept it a secret. Ronald was afraid that everyone at the bank would find out and it would hurt our careers. Then he dumped me and I figured that he never really cared for me anyway."

"And now he's in town?"

"Yeah. In fact, you saw him that day outside the coffee shop. He was talking to me when you came out, remember?"

Liam slowly let the breath seep from his lungs. God, how could he have been so stupid? Ellie hadn't looked a thing like her picture, why had he expected Ronald Pettibone to resemble his photo? Maybe it was all part of the plan, Liam mused. A new life, a new look. But Ellie was living her life out in the open. She was looking for a new job and making new friends and in no way trying to hide her identity. Not the behavior of someone just one step in front of the law.

But could the same be said for Ronald Pettibone? Not for one instant did Liam believe his appearance in Boston was coincidental. He'd come to her for a reason and either it was the money they'd both stolen or it was Ellie herself. Whichever it turned out to be, Liam wasn't going to be a happy man.

"Maybe you should call him back," Liam suggested.

"Now?"

"Not this minute. But after you get out of the tub."

Ellie slowly swirled her hand around in the water.

"It's all over between Ronald and me. I don't want you to think that—"

"I don't," Liam interrupted, already learning to hate the guy's name. Ronald. Ronald was the name of the weaselly kid who was the tattletale in grade school. Ronald was the name of the brainiac in high school who always got a better grade in English. And Ronald was the kind of guy you just wanted to punch in the nose.

Liam grabbed the mug and began to rinse the soap out of Ellie's hair. For a long time they didn't speak. He wasn't sure what to say. Hell, he knew Ellie had a past with men, far fewer than the number of women he'd had in his life. But Ronald Pettibone wasn't just any old boyfriend. If he and Ellie had pulled off a crime together, then they shared a connection a little deeper than just physical attraction.

He bit back a curse, stood and grabbed a towel from the stand next to the sink. "The water is getting cold," he said.

Ellie stared at him for a long moment, as if she were trying to read his expression. Then she slowly stood, the water sluicing off her naked body. Liam quickly wrapped her in the towel, unwilling to tempt himself any further. He was this close to dragging her down to the bathroom floor to really make love to her.

"You're not angry that he called, are you?"

"Why would you think that?" Liam asked, tucking the towel tight around her breasts.

"You just seemed a little...perturbed."

It wouldn't do to have Ellie suspicious, Liam mused. But he wasn't about to deny his feelings. "Maybe I am, a little. But that shouldn't stop you from seeing him. He said something about banks. Maybe he can help you find a new job."

A slow smile curved Ellie's lips. "I never thought about that. He said he had some contacts here in Boston. Maybe he can give me a few leads. In fact, that's probably what he wants to talk to me about."

"Why don't you finish drying off and I'll go get us some lunch?" Liam said. "I'll pick up a couple of sandwiches and we'll just relax."

"The sun's come out," Ellie said. "Maybe we should go out to lunch and then go sight-seeing. I'm feeling much better now. And the fresh air and exercise will do me good."

In truth, Liam was anxious to get out of the apartment so he could give Sean the news. Ronald Pettibone was in town and Liam knew exactly where to find him. If things went well, Liam would have answers to all his questions soon. And then he'd finally know exactly where he stood with Ellie Thorpe.

5

THE BAPTISM BRUNCH was already in full swing by the time Sean arrived. Liam watched him walk through the door of Conor and Olivia's apartment. In truth, Liam hadn't expected his brother to show up since Fiona was going to be in attendance. When he'd left their flat, Sean had been lying on the sofa, watching a basketball game.

The relationship between Liam's long-lost mother and her son had grown more and more strained since she'd come back into their lives, and Sean avoided her presence whenever he could. Liam hadn't minded that Sean might not show up. He had been hoping to get at least a little break from his brother's constant concern about their case.

Liam glanced over at Ellie. She was standing near the baby-buggy-shaped cake, chatting with Brendan's fiancée, Amy. He had wondered how Ellie would get along at a Quinn family gathering, considering that his family could be a bit overwhelming at times. And he almost hadn't asked her to come. But then he'd decided it would be easier to keep an eye on her if he just kept her close.

Bringing a date to a family function had caused more than a few raised eyebrows, but no one commented out loud. Liam's sister, Keely, had come up first, introducing herself to Ellie, then motioning her husband, Rafe, over to join the conversation. It had been a year since their wedding and though Rafe and the Quinns had had issues in the past, everyone could see that he made Keely very happy. Along with Olivia, Meggie and Amy, Rafe had become part of the ever-expanding Quinn clan.

Olivia and Conor wandered among the guests, introducing their son, Conor smiling from ear to ear and Olivia looking more beautiful than ever. They came up to Amy and Ellie, and a moment later Ellie had the baby in her arms. Liam's breath caught in his throat as he saw her smile sweetly at Riley, then kiss the soft dusting of hair on his head.

No matter how much time had passed, Liam was still amazed by the circumstances that had brought them together. Had he seen her sipping a drink at Quinn's Pub or walking along any sidewalk in Boston, he probably wouldn't have given Ellie a second look. But something had happened to him when she'd hit him over the head with that lamp, something that had jarred loose in his brain, and by the end of that night he'd become completely smitten.

"Will you look at this?" Brendan muttered, walking up behind Liam. "Sean decided to put in an appearance. Conor told me he wasn't coming."

Sean stopped short when Fiona approached, then deftly turned and headed toward the table. But he was halted again, this time by someone Sean hadn't expected—Ellie Thorpe. Liam winced and knew that he was about to catch holy hell.

"Maybe you should introduce him to your new girl-friend," Brendan suggested.

"She's not my girlfriend. Besides—"

"What the hell is she doing here?" Sean murmured under his breath as he approached Liam.

Liam grabbed Brendan's plate. "Looks like you could use a little more to eat, Bren," he said. "I'll just go get us a few of those sandwiches." He headed for the tiny kitchen, but Sean just followed him, cornering Liam at the refrigerator.

"Answer my question," Sean demanded.

Liam snatched up two sandwiches and shoved one at Sean. "Have something to eat and relax," he muttered.

His brother tossed the sandwich back onto the plate.

"That's really good chicken salad," Liam said. "You should try it."

"I told you to get close to her. But I didn't mean this close." He gave Liam a shrewd look. "Are you sleeping with her?"

"Not right now. I'm talking to you and thinking that I might just have a few of those shrimp over there. Con and Olivia really went all out here, didn't they? This is quite a spread."

"Do you think this is funny?"

"No," Liam replied with a low chuckle. "But I didn't have much choice in the matter. I think some-one is trying to kill her."

Sean gasped, then grabbed Liam's arm and dragged him out to the small porch off the kitchen. The sky was gray and a light mist hung over the city. "What hap-pened?" he asked.

"A lot of things," Liam replied, glancing back over his shoulder to make sure no one could overhear. "And all of them pretty strange. First, there was the burglary. Then Ellie told me she nearly got hit on the head by a brick falling off her apartment roof. And then, yesterday, she almost got run down by a car just outside her apartment building. The burglary might have been random, but that car was aiming for her."

"Did you get a plate on the car?"

"Yeah." Liam reached into the pocket of his sports jacket and pulled out the two photos he'd developed that morning. "I enlarged these and you can see there's a rental sticker on the back bumper. I went to the place, but they wouldn't give me any information about who rented the car."

"I'll see what I can find. If they won't tell me, maybe I can get Conor to give me some help."

"Listen," Liam said. "I don't know who Ellie is or what she's done, but I do know that if I don't keep an eye on her, she might just end up dead. So don't give me any grief, all right?"

"All right," Sean said. "But from now on I'm keeping an eye on you while you keep an eye on her."

"Here you are!" Liam and Sean turned to find Ellie in the doorway. The cool breeze ruffled her hair and, at that moment, Liam hadn't seen anything quite as eautiful as Ellie in his whole life.

"Ellie, this is my brother Sean," Liam said. "Sean, El Thorpe. She lives over in Charlestown. She's new to b   on."

Ellie   out her hand and Sean reluctantly took it. "Pleasure,

"I'm not sure I'm ever going to remember all these names," she said with a warm smile. "You all look so much alike, the dark hair and the...eyes."

"Right," Sean said.

As usual, in the presence of a woman, Sean didn't have much to say. He shoved his hands into his pockets and watched them both with an uneasy smile. "So, how did you two meet?"

"Liam saved me from a burglar who'd broken into my apartment."

Sean nodded, as if he were really interested. Then he shrugged. "I gotta go."

"It was nice to meet you," Ellie said.

"Nice meeting you."

They watched him walk back inside the apartment, then Liam turned to Ellie. "Don't worry about him. He's a little shy."

"You mean, not all the Quinns are as charming as you?"

"Sean has his own special way with women. He ignores them and they can't seem to resist the challenge." Liam slipped his arm around Ellie's shoulders. "Are you ready to go? I think I've snapped enough photos to fill a few albums. No one can say I shirked my family responsibilities."

"We don't have to go. The food looks good. And Olivia was going to show me the gifts she got for the baby." She held up her champagne flute. "And I'm going to have another mimosa."

"I'll get you one," Liam said, dropping a quick kiss on her lips. He was tempted to linger, but knew that they'd already generated enough curiosity without adding more fodder for speculation to the mix. He left Ellie in the kitchen when she offered to help Olivia slice more baked ham for sandwiches. The champagne was on ice in the dining room and he found Sean staring at the cake, a perplexed expression on his face.

"What is this?" he asked.

"A cake."

"I know it's a cake."

"It's a baby buggy."

"I thought it was a clam with wheels."

"Don't let Olivia hear that. Conor said she spent two days making that." Liam glanced over at his brother, considering what he was going to say to him next. He'd thought about his options over and over again over the past few days, trying to decide how to handle the situation. "There is one more thing I should tell you," Liam murmured. "Ronald Pettibone is in town."

Sean's head snapped around, his attention focused.

"He's been in Boston for about a week," Liam continued. "That was him outside the coffee shop—the guy I mentioned who was arguing with her."

"How do you know?"

"She told me. He looks different from the photo. He's not wearing his glasses anymore and he's changed his hair. It's lighter. And he has a tan, too. He's staying at the Bostonian, Room 215. Pretty ritzy digs for a guy who is out of work, don't you think?"

"How did you find all this out?"

"He left a message on her machine while I was at her apartment."

"Was she there?"

"Of course she was," Liam said. "We were... together."

Sean sent him a suspicious look. "How did she react?"

"It was a little hard to see, since she had her back to me. But I encouraged her to call him back and she said she would. Until then, I think you should keep an eye on the guy. And find out if he rented a black sedan a few days ago."

"You think *he* tried to run her down? Then she's got to be mixed up in this. What motive would he have to kill her? Unless he didn't want to split the take."

"He's her ex-lover. Maybe he's obsessed," Liam replied. "Just keep an eye on him." He paused, wondering about his next move. He reached into his pocket and pulled out a set of keys. "Here."

"What's this?"

"It's the keys to Ellie's apartment. I put in a new security system for her in case Pettibone came calling again. The code is 3-5-5-4. Make sure you get it right or you'll set off the alarm."

"All right," Sean said. "Three-five-five-four."

"I've got tickets to the Sox home opener on Tuesday. I'm supposed to photograph the mayor doing some pregame presentation and then he's going to throw out the first pitch. None of their sports guys want to do it, so they hired me. I'm taking Ellie. She should be safe in a stadium full of thirty-six thousand people."

"Good. That should give me plenty of time."

Liam's jaw went tight. "Just don't make a mess, all right? I don't want her to be all upset again."

Sean nodded.

Satisfied that the matter had been taken out of his hands, Liam sighed. "I'm going to go talk to Ma. Why don't you come with me?"

"Nah, not today."

"Why not today? It's as good a time as any. Sean, you can't carry this grudge any longer. Da has forgiven her. So has Keely—and they had a whole lot more to be pissed about than you and me."

"She walked out on us, Li. You were just a baby and I was three years old. She says she had to get away and she did. But why didn't she come back?"

"Why don't you ask her?"

"Because I don't want to hear her answer."

Liam shrugged. "Suit yourself." With that he grabbed a bottle of champagne and decided to find Ellie. Right now he needed to hear her voice, to remember what they'd shared together in her bathroom and how good it felt to touch her. He didn't need to worry about whether he was lusting after a criminal or whether her boyfriend was out to cause her harm.

He caught Ellie's gaze from across the room and motioned her to meet him near the front door. She sent him a coy smile and then a tiny frown, but Liam wasn't about to give up. He slipped out of the apartment, leaned up against the wall and waited for her. A few seconds later she poked her head out the door. He reached over and grabbed her, pulling her out into the hall, the door slamming behind her.

"Come on," he murmured, heading for the stairs. They walked down two flights until they reached the street. Liam shrugged out of his jacket and draped it around Ellie's shoulders as they stepped outside. After they sat down on the front stoop, he popped the cork on the champagne bottle. "I didn't bring glasses," he said. "We'll have to drink from the bottle."

Liam took a sip, then handed the bottle to Ellie. She tipped it up, but the champagne bubbled in her mouth. She wrinkled her nose as she swallowed, then coughed softly. Liam used the opportunity to pull her into his arms. "I should never have brought you here," he said, pressing his mouth against her neck.

"Why is that?"

"Because I prefer to kiss you whenever I feel like kissing you."

"Then you'd better get kissing," Ellie teased, "because if we stay out here too long, we'll be missed."

Liam pulled back and looked down into her pretty face. There were times when he felt he could see into the corners of her soul. And then, other times, he wondered if he was just fooling himself. But as he captured her mouth with his, tasting the sweet champagne, all of his doubts seemed to dissolve. For now, Ellie was simply the woman who made his blood run hot and his heart pound hard.

For now, that was enough.

"NOW YOU'RE A TRUE Bostonian," Liam said, tugging on the brim of Ellie's brand new Boston Red Sox cap. "You've been to Fenway and seen someone hit a home run over the big Green Monster. Unfortunately, it wasn't one of our players."

She stared out the front window of his car as they waited for the light to change. "I've never been much of a baseball fan. In New York, you have to choose sides—Mets or Yankees. I never knew enough about baseball, so I stayed neutral and didn't get involved."

"I've loved baseball since I was a kid," Liam said, turning the car onto Charlestown Avenue. "I remember the first time I went to Fenway, I must have been about seven or eight. I walked in and it was so green. We'd come from Southie on the T and it was the middle of a heat wave. Our neighborhood was dry and dusty and everything was faded by the sun. And then we walked into Fenway and it was like an oasis—although I didn't know what an oasis was back then."

"Did you go to a lot of games as a kid?" Ellie asked.

"No. We didn't have the money for tickets. But Conor had a couple of buddies who sold popcorn at the park, and if the crowd was thin, they'd let us in before the seventh inning stretch. We never got to see a complete game, but we'd hang around outside afterward and get the players to sign our baseball cards."

"Sounds like fun," Ellie said.

"It was. We didn't have much, but we always had fun." He chuckled softly. "When I first saw Fenway, I thought it was Ireland."

"What?"

"I'd always heard my older brothers and father talking about how green Ireland was. They were all born there. And Fenway was the greenest thing I'd ever seen, so I thought it was Ireland. I wasn't ever good with geography, at least not in second grade."

Ellie nodded. "When I was a kid, I used to think that my teachers lived at the school. That they all slept together in a little room somewhere and talked about books and chalk and school paste all day and all night.

I figured that's why I never saw them around town. They weren't allowed out."

Liam turned his car onto Ellie's street and scanned the length of it for a place to park. He found a spot right in front, and when he shut the car off, he waited for her to ask him in. Since their encounter in the bathroom, they'd both been a bit hesitant about where to go next. Though Liam didn't regret what they'd done, he had to admit that the event had brought a change in his feelings toward her.

With other women such an intimacy had always signaled the start of a very passionate but brief affair. With Ellie he was afraid to repeat what they'd shared, afraid that he'd have just a finite number of nights with her before it was all over. He'd have to use them sparingly.

Liam hadn't given a thought to the future. Until he knew who'd embezzled the money from Ellie's bank, then he couldn't completely believe that she hadn't. And allowing himself to get wrapped up in her life right now was not a smart move.

"Do you want to come in?" Ellie asked.

He'd refused after he'd taken her to the baptism brunch, but it would be difficult to say no again without her wondering why. "Sure. For a little while. I gave the film to one of the sports guys before we left Fenway, so I just have to go down to the *Globe* before seven to look at the proofs."

"I'll make us some hot chocolate and we can warm up."

They strolled up to her building, then climbed the stairs to the third floor. But when she reached her front door, Ellie stopped short. The door was ajar. She reached out and pushed it open, but Liam slipped around her side and stepped in first.

"What happened here?" Ellie murmured, peering over his shoulder.

It was apparent to Liam that the apartment had been torn apart from top to bottom, completely ransacked. He held his arm out to keep her behind him. "Just wait," he murmured. "Stay right here."

"You think he's still here?" Ellie asked with a gasp.

Liam slowly walked through the apartment, checking each room and flipping on lights, finding them all in the same condition as the others. When he was satisfied that they were alone, he carefully evaluated the scene. He wasn't really sure what to look for. Sean was the P.I. and Conor was the cop. He was completely out of his element here.

He walked back out into the living room to find Ellie sitting on the edge of the sofa, still in shock. "Is anything missing?"

"How am I supposed to tell?" Ellie asked with a defeated shrug.

"Well, let's just start to pick everything up and put it in its place and maybe you'll notice if something is missing." He sighed. "I guess we shouldn't touch anything until the police take a look first."

"No," she said, jumping to her feet. "I don't want to pick this up. I don't want to hang around until the police arrive. I don't want to stay here. This is the second time someone has come into this apartment and I don't feel safe here anymore. We have to leave."

"I can't understand how they got in without setting off the security alarm."

Ellie gnawed her bottom lip as she glanced furtively over at the keypad he'd so patiently explained to her.

"You didn't set the alarm?"

"I was in a hurry and you were waiting. We were late for the game."

Liam closed his eyes and sighed deeply. "Well, at least you weren't here."

"And I'm not going be here tonight, either. I'll find a hotel—with big locks on the door and a burly security guard in the lobby."

"No," Liam said. "I'll take you somewhere safe. You can come home with me."

Ellie blinked, clearly surprised by his offer. "I couldn't do that."

Liam glanced around the apartment again, a thought creeping into his mind. Sean had a key. Had he done this to Ellie's apartment? Liam couldn't believe his brother would be so obvious—unless he meant to scare Ellie on purpose. Now he was glad they hadn't called the police.

"You can," Liam said. He pulled her into his arms, pressing his lips to her forehead.

Ellie sank against his body and he held her gently, stroking her back. "Maybe I'm just not meant to live in Boston. Maybe I should go somewhere else. I was reading this book the other day that said—"

Before she could continue Liam brought his mouth down on hers, stopping her words in her throat. The kiss was soft and reassuring and Ellie opened beneath his gentle assault. She smoothed her hands over his face as he kissed her, exploring with her fingertips, her touch heating his blood.

He pulled back and smiled down at her. "We can talk about books later," he said. "Why don't you go grab what you need and we'll go over to my place? Tomorrow we'll come back and clean up."

Ellie nodded. "Thank you."

"For what?"

"For being here. For watching out for me."

Liam waited while she packed, walking through her apartment and picking up where he could. When he found the phone beneath a pillow from the sofa, he put the receiver back into the cradle. He was tempted to call Sean but he'd leave that for later.

Ellie reappeared a few minutes later with a small duffel bag. "He went through my dresser," she said. "But he didn't touch my jewelry." She paused, then shook her head. "No, it couldn't be him."

"Who?"

"I'm just being paranoid."

"Who?" Liam demanded, slipping the strap of her bag from her shoulder. He reset the alarm, then closed the door behind them and locked the dead bolt. They walked down the stairs to the street and Ellie stopped. "Ronald," she finally said.

Liam wasn't sure how he ought to react. Either Ellie was genuinely confused by all that had happened or she was very deftly throwing suspicion onto her partner in crime. "Ronald Pettibone?"

"I just don't know…" she said, shaking her head.

"Why would you think it could be him?"

"He broke up with me. And he was pretty clear that

he didn't want to remain friends. That's why I left the bank. And then, out of the blue, he shows up here. He claimed to have friends here, but we spent a long weekend in Boston about a month before we broke up and he didn't mention any friends then. Do you think he's stalking me?"

"I don't know," Liam said. "But I'll find out."

Liam glanced up and down the street before they got into his car, noticing a black sedan with tinted windows parked down the block. Now *he* was feeling a little paranoid.

As they drove through the city, he kept his eyes on the rearview mirror, swinging around the block every now and then to make sure he wasn't being followed. When he was satisfied that the black sedan wasn't tailing them, he headed toward Southie.

He hoped that Sean would be gone when he got home, but when he stepped inside his flat, he found both Sean and Brian sitting on the sofa, eating pizza and watching a game show. They both registered surprise at seeing Ellie again, but for completely different reasons.

"Hey there, Ellie," Brian said, standing and brushing the crumbs off the front of his sweater. "It's nice to see you again. How was the game?"

"It was great," she said, giving him a warm smile. "The Red Sox lost, but it was still fun."

Liam ignored a tiny sliver of jealousy as Brian held on to her hand for just a bit too long. "You know, if you spend much more time at our place, you're going to have to start paying rent," he told Brian.

"I'll remember that next time you come over to do your laundry for free."

Sean pushed to his feet. "What are you two doing here?"

"Someone broke into Ellie's apartment," Liam said.

"Again," Ellie added.

"Again?" Brian asked. "You've had more than one break-in? Gee, Charlestown doesn't have a real high burglary rate. Do you think there's some kind of crime wave starting there?"

"I think I'm being stalked," Ellie said. "That, or I'm really unlucky."

"Ellie is going to stay here until we figure out what's going on with her apartment." Liam took her arm and tugged her along to his room. "Why don't you get settled? Then we'll go out and get some dinner." He closed the bedroom door behind her, then strode over to the sofa. "Did you ransack her apartment?" he demanded, his voice a harsh whisper.

"No," Sean said. "I went though everything, but I put it all back in place before I left. Someone must have been there after me. It wouldn't have been too hard for him to get in—I couldn't reset the alarm because it wasn't set in the first place. Ellie might have noticed."

"This wouldn't have happened if you'd been watching him like you were supposed to," Liam said.

"Wait a second here," Brian interrupted. "Sean broke into her apartment?"

"No, I had a key," Sean said. "The other guy broke in."

"How'd you get a key?"

"Liam gave it to me."

Brian frowned. "I'm seriously out of the loop here, aren't I?"

"It's a case we're working on," Liam said.

"Ellie's an embezzler," Sean commented.

Liam bristled. "She is not."

"She might be," Sean snapped.

Brian got to his feet and grabbed his jacket from the end of the sofa. "I don't think I want to be in the middle of this. I'm going down to the pub to have a pint of the black stuff. Guinness always seems to clear the head. There should be a pretty good party going on there now after the game. Da is serving free hot dogs."

"I'll go with you," Sean said.

"No way," Liam said. "You'll go figure out what Ronald Pettibone is up to. Did you trace that license plate I gave you? I know he was the one who tried to run Ellie down."

"Someone tried to run down Ellie?" Brian asked. "Forget the Guinness. This sounds like a good story."

Sean grabbed his twin brother's arm. "You're always sniffin' for a story, aren't you?" Sean muttered. "Come on, I'll let you drive. Let's see if we can find this Ronald Pettibone."

"And don't come back tonight," Liam warned. "Sleep at Brian's." When they'd both walked out the door, Liam flopped onto the sofa and grabbed a piece of pizza, munching on it distractedly. How the hell was he supposed to keep Ellie safe if Sean didn't do his part? This was his case and here he was, feet up on the coffee table, eating pizza when he should have been out doing his job.

Liam tipped his head back. There were moments

when he cursed the day he'd decided to help with this case and his impulse to ride to Ellie Thorpe's rescue. Now it seemed he was pulling her out of harm's way nearly every day.

"I'm doomed," Liam murmured. If this wasn't enough to bring the Quinn family curse raining down on his head, he wasn't sure what was. He and Ellie might as well start picking out the china and monogramming the towels. Marriage couldn't be far behind.

ELLIE STARED at her reflection in the bathroom mirror, then forced a smile. A nervous knot tightened in her stomach and she wondered if it might be better to just stay in the bathroom until morning. But then the bathroom at her place had been the scene of their last intimate encounter. Perhaps the hall closet here at Liam's might be a better choice.

She smoothed her hands over the Patriots jersey that Liam had given her to wear to bed. Like a fool, she'd brought everything she'd needed—except a nightgown. And the last thing she wanted Liam to think was that she'd done it on purpose in the hope that a naked body in his bed might be too tempting to resist.

Ellie groaned softly. Sex. That's what this was all about. If the opportunity presented itself, how could she refuse? Liam was just too much to resist. But her past troubles with men still nagged at her. What had she done wrong? Had she been too aggressive or maybe not aggressive enough? Had her skills in the bedroom been a disappointment? Ellie stretched the jersey tight across her breasts. Maybe it was her body.

She'd only have one chance with Liam and she didn't want to blow it. He was the kind of man who would bring out her passionate nature. He made her feel sexy and uninhibited and a little bit naughty. She glanced down at the sink and her stomach did a little flip as she remembered that afternoon in her bathroom.

Their first intimate encounter had been...overwhelming. She wasn't sure she'd be able to remain conscious for anything more exciting than that! Taking a deep breath, she raked her fingers through her hair, then turned for the door. When she stepped out, she found Liam smoothing a sheet over the sofa.

She pasted a smile on her face. They hadn't discussed sleeping arrangements, but it was obvious that they wouldn't be sharing his bed. She tried to hide her disappointment. "You don't need to do that. I can fix it."

Liam shrugged. "I'll sleep out here. You can have my bed."

Ellie reached out and took the pillow from his hands. "No, don't be silly. I'll be fine here. I don't want to put you out."

"All right," he said softly, clearly uneasy with the discussion. "But if you need anything, I'll be close by." He sent her a sideways glance and, in that instant, Ellie saw the desire in his eyes. But for some reason he'd chosen not to act on that desire tonight. What had changed?

Liam reached out, hooked a finger under her chin, then gave her a quick kiss. "Sleep tight," he murmured. "I'll see you in the morning." With that he turned and walked into his bedroom, closing the door behind him.

Ellie sat on the sofa and pulled a down comforter around her shoulders. Things had been going so well. Though they hadn't spent a night in bed together, she sensed that their relationship was moving forward. But now it had come to a full stop.

"He's just another man," she muttered, reaching for the light. She flopped down on the sofa and pulled the comforter up to her chin. "Nothing special."

She pinched her eyes closed, but as she tried to relax, her head spun with thoughts of Liam. She settled on an image of him lying in his bed, naked, the sheet low on his waist. She'd never seen him completely naked, but Ellie knew what was beneath the shirt—a broad chest and narrow waist, muscled arms and a smooth back. She could almost feel his skin beneath her fingers and she clenched her hands into fists to banish the sensation. And she could certainly guess at what was beneath the jeans.

Though she tried everything she could to relax, nothing worked. At first she thought it was the upset over her apartment, but after considering all that had happened during the day, Ellie decided that the reason she couldn't sleep was lying in a bed just a few short steps away.

After an hour of tossing and turning, Ellie threw the comforter off and sat up, cursing softly in the dark. She walked to the small kitchen at the back of the flat and pulled open the freezer door. When she couldn't sleep, a pint of gourmet ice cream always did the trick.

"Oh, my," Ellie murmured. Half the freezer was stacked with frozen pizza and the other half with a variety of ice creams. She pulled one carton out after another. "Rocky Road, French Vanilla, Cookies and Cream." Ellie grabbed another carton. "O-oh, Chocolate Chip Mint. I love that." She rummaged through the drawers until she found a spoon, then opened the first carton, leaving the freezer door ajar so she could gaze at her selection.

Ellie had never trusted herself with more than one pint of ice cream in her freezer at a time. The temptation was just too great and ice cream was her drug of choice when she felt depressed about her social life. She opened the carton of Rocky Road and scooped out a spoonful, then let it melt in her mouth.

"This is better than sex," she murmured.

"Couldn't sleep?"

A tiny cry slipped from Ellie's lips, as she spun around, her spoon clattering to the floor. Liam stood in the kitchen, wearing only a pair of boxer shorts that rode low on his hips. A wave of mortification washed over her and she quickly turned and stuck the ice cream back in the freezer. "Sorry," she murmured. "I just thought something to eat would…"

He raked his hand through his dark hair. "No, it's all right." He reached around her, his chest brushing against her arm, the heat of his skin against hers making Ellie feel a bit dizzy. "I came out for the same thing."

He grabbed the open carton and handed it back to her, then selected Chocolate Chip Mint for himself. Ellie handed him a clean spoon. Liam scooped a spoonful out of the carton and held it out to her. Hesitantly, Ellie leaned forward and let the ice cream slide onto her tongue to melt in her mouth.

"Mmm. Good," she said.

Liam grinned, then took a bite himself. "What do you have?"

He reached over and scooped out some Rocky Road and held it out to her. But as she took the spoon into her mouth, a bit of melted ice cream dribbled down her chin. Liam reached out and caught it, then held his finger in front of Ellie's lips.

She took his finger in her mouth and only then realized what she was doing. Ellie glanced up at him and slowly pulled back. "Yum," she said, her voice cracking slightly.

They stared at each other for a long moment and Ellie held her breath, waiting, wondering what would happen next. Then suddenly, Liam tossed the carton to the floor, grabbed her Rocky Road and threw it down, as well. In an instant his hands were on her body, cupping her face, spanning her waist, slipping beneath the football jersey and smoothing over her bare skin.

He kissed her as if only her mouth could satisfy his hunger, delving deep, tasting fully. Ellie's head spun and her limbs felt weak, his kiss like a drug, wiping away the last traces of inhibitions. She'd never wanted a man as much as she wanted Liam. The need was so intense, it frightened her. His lips moved to her throat and Ellie tipped her head back, sighing softly. Her fingers furrowed through his hair and she sank against him.

Skimming her hands over his chest, she reveled in the way he was made. She'd always admired the male physique but had never experienced a man quite as perfect as Liam Quinn. Every inch of his body was taut and toned, muscle and sinew covered by smooth skin.

When he pulled away for a moment, Ellie took the chance to explore. She kissed the hollow at the base of his neck, the few soft hairs there tickling her lips. Then she marked a trail across his chest with her tongue, circling his nipple. She didn't want to leave any doubt at all about what she needed from him.

He sighed softly and Ellie pressed her body against his as his mouth came down on hers again. She felt his need, hard and hot through the thin silk of his boxer shorts. With deliberate intent, she moved her hips, tempting him with pleasures that they had yet to share. He couldn't refuse her. Every movement, every subtle reaction, told her that he wouldn't.

Ellie had never considered herself a highly sexual woman, but with Liam her inhibitions seemed to vanish. She wanted him, his body above her, beneath her and inside her. She wanted to lose herself in the rhythm of their joining and then experience his release, the ultimate surrender. Yet she couldn't bring herself to ask out loud.

She moved her hand along his belly but he grabbed her fingers at the last moment and brought them back up to his chest. "We should go to bed," he murmured, his breath ragged against her ear.

A stab of disappointment shot through her. But then Ellie realized that maybe he was offering her an invitation, not calling an end to this seduction. She took a shaky breath and swallowed hard. "Your bed or mine?"

6

LIAM GAZED DOWN into Ellie's eyes, watching the doubts and insecurities flicker there. He couldn't deny the need he had, this irrational yet overwhelming desire to possess her body. But it wasn't just a physical need, a desire to lose himself in warmth. He didn't want just any woman. He wanted Ellie Thorpe.

In his mind there was no other woman, no one more beautiful or clever or interesting just over the horizon. He'd reached the horizon and he'd found a woman who satisfied him in every way. And now he wanted to satisfy her. But he felt as if he were out of his league. This wasn't just sex anymore. It was something new...unfamiliar...and completely unexpected. "Are you sure?" he murmured.

A tiny smile touched her lips and she ran her hand down his chest, her fingers leaving a warm trail on his skin. "That I want you? Yes, I'm sure. I don't think I've ever been more sure of anything in my life. If you're sure, that is."

Liam hooked a finger under her chin and forced her gaze away from a careful study of his chest. She looked up at him, wide-eyed. "I'm sure," he said.

Ellie frowned. "We are talking about sex, right? And not about sleeping in the same bed?"

"One usually follows the other," Liam replied. "But that was my interpretation of the conversation."

Ellie sighed softly. "Good. All right. So that's settled, then. I think you should take me back to bed."

God, she was sweet. He loved how she just spoke her mind, refusing to play the coy little games that had been so common with women in his past. It wasn't hard to know what Ellie Thorpe was thinking. She usually said it the moment it raced through her head. Liam reached out and slipped his hands around her waist, tugging her near.

He bunched the hem of the football jersey in his fists as he kissed her again, lingering over her lips, giving her a chance to respond. Unlike their last encounter, Liam was determined to take it slow this time, to enjoy every moment...every caress...every long, deep kiss.

A tiny sigh slipped from her throat and Liam felt his control waver. In truth, he wondered if he'd have any control at all once they reached the bedroom. Maybe they should just stay in the kitchen. The bathroom had been good in the past and the kitchen also worked well. But, in the end, Liam picked her up and carried her to his bedroom, her legs wrapped around his waist, her backside cupped in his hands.

Liam had never brought a woman to his own bed. It had been an unwritten rule of his, far easier to leave her place than his. But now all the rules seemed to be falling by the wayside with Ellie—and Liam was glad to see them go.

He set her softly on the bed, then reached down and tugged the Patriots jersey over her head. His breath caught in his throat as he looked at her, her narrow shoulders and her perfect breasts, the way her skin shone in the light from the moon filtering through the bedroom window. Slowly he reached out and ran his hand over her shoulder and down her arm. Ellie caught his fingers in hers and gently pulled him down on top of her.

He was already hard and ready and Liam knew he'd have to be careful. And when Ellie reached to run her hand over his shaft, her fingers warm through the silk of his boxers, Liam knew he was lost. He groaned and she took it as encouragement, wrapping her fingers around him. Suddenly he was grateful for the barrier of fabric between her touch and his need.

He pressed his mouth against her neck and then her shoulder, slowly moving down her body, exploring her flesh with his mouth. Her nipple peaked as he teased at it with his tongue. But this time she didn't give over to her own passion, but matched him kiss for kiss, caress for caress.

They took turns, each of them slowly tracing a map of seduction over limbs and down bellies, around nipples and under earlobes. He'd never taken such time with foreplay, but Liam found himself more aroused than he'd ever been before, constantly teetering near the edge of release.

Through it all, she spoke to him, moaning his name, teasing him, telling him what she liked and asking him what he wanted. At first Liam had been uneasy voicing his needs, but after a while it became so arousing that he couldn't help himself.

When he slipped his hand beneath her panties, she

moaned softly. "Oh, yes," she said, her words coming out on a breath. "Oh, there."

While he touched her, Ellie's fingers delved beneath the waistband of his boxers. As he found the damp entrance between her legs, she stroked his hard shaft, her touch cool and tantalizing against his heat. Liam knew if he just let himself ride the wave of sensation that he'd find his release in her hand. But that wasn't where he wanted things to end. There was so much to share with Ellie and, tonight, he wanted it all.

"Slow," he murmured. "God, Ellie, I'm too close."

Determined to continue, Liam had no choice but to stop the torment. He grabbed her around the waist and pulled her on top of him. Then, he fixed his gaze on hers and slowly skimmed his hands over her body. Ellie smiled at him, leaned forward and kissed him, her breasts brushing against his chest, her nipples hard. "Tell me what you want," she murmured.

"You. All of you."

"I think we might be overdressed."

"Maybe you're right."

With a sly smile, Ellie hooked her fingers around the waistband of his boxers and slowly tugged them down over his hips, sliding back as she pulled until she sat at his feet. And then she moved back up, sliding her body along his legs. When her breasts brushed against his erection, Liam moaned softly. But then Ellie backtracked and began to tease him with her lips and tongue.

Liam tried to keep a grip on his control, but this new torment was almost too much to bear. "Ellie, don't."

Still, it was as if she could read his reactions, knowing just when to slow or to stop her gentle assault. She caressed him with her mouth and he arched toward her, lost in a wild storm of sensation. And then she would retreat, leaving him hanging on the edge, his desire building until it threatened to explode without warning. "Oh, Ellie. Don't do that," he murmured.

But she didn't heed his request, taking him closer to the edge again, then letting him slip back. It was as if she wanted to prove herself to him, to return the pleasure that he'd given her that night in the bathroom. Her hair tickled his belly as she continued her sensual torture and Liam clenched his teeth, sucking in a sharp breath and holding it. And just when he didn't think he could stand another second of torment, she stopped.

A moment later she was lying beside him, her body curled against his. Ellie kissed his shoulder. "I'm feeling a little tired," she teased. "Maybe we should go to sleep now."

Liam growled playfully, then pulled her beneath him. "You're the kind of woman my da warned me about," he said, pressing his hips against hers, his erection hot on her belly.

"Do you always listen to your da?" she asked.

"Never," Liam said.

"Then make love to me, Liam Quinn."

Liam opened the drawer of the bedside table, grabbed a box of condoms and handed them to her. "We should probably take care of this first."

She pulled out a foil package and tore it open with her teeth, then slowly sheathed him, turning it into a little game. Liam felt a knot of desire tighten in his belly. He slid her panties down, and when she'd kicked them off her feet, he knew he couldn't wait any longer. He pulled her back on top of him, anxious to bury himself in her warmth.

Ellie bent and kissed him, sliding along the length of his shaft as she did. Liam grabbed her hips to keep her from moving. But Ellie wasn't content to wait. She rose on her knees and then slowly came down on top of him, taking him inside her until he was buried to the hilt. A soft sigh slipped from her lips and she closed her eyes, settling herself above him.

They stayed like that for a long moment and Liam watched as a smile curved the corners of her mouth. He felt the knot tighten and he reached between them and touched her. Ellie's smile intensified and she began to move, slowly at first and then with greater abandon.

Liam's pulse pounded in his head and he lost himself in the feel of her body, the wet heat driving him closer and closer to his release. Every thought was focused on their joining, every nerve poised to explode. He wanted to possess her, completely, to touch her soul and share her release.

Though instinct drove him, Liam was still acutely aware of what he was feeling. And it was like nothing he'd ever experienced before. Their joining was beyond just two bodies engaged in the heat of the moment. They'd stripped away the barriers and they were two souls merging into one.

Ellie moaned softly, then murmured his name. Liam knew she was near her own orgasm and he wanted to wait and experience it before taking his own release.

But then she was there, contracting around him, and Liam knew he couldn't wait.

He murmured her name, spanning her waist with his hands and driving into her one last time. His release was so shattering, so intense, that he wasn't sure it would ever end. Spasms of pleasure rocked his body and he lost all sense of who he was and what he was doing.

And when Ellie finally collapsed on top of him, he ran his fingers through the hair at her nape and tried to slow his breathing. It had never, ever, been like this before. He wanted to tell her that, to make her understand what they had shared, but he couldn't find the words.

"You're the kind of man my grandmother warned me about," Ellie murmured, nuzzling her face into her neck.

"And what kind is that?"

She pressed her palms against his chest and smiled down at him. "The kind of man who makes me forget what a good girl I am."

"You are a good girl," Liam said. "But you can be very, very bad."

Ellie giggled. "And I can be a lot worse. Just give me a few minutes to recover."

SHE FELT HIS LIPS on her shoulder and then on her neck. Ellie slowly opened her eyes to the morning light. Liam lay next to her in bed, dressed in jeans and a T-shirt. A tiny smile curved the corners of her mouth as she stared into his eyes. "Morning," she murmured.

"Morning," he said, stealing a quick kiss.

"What time is it?"

"A little after nine. Go back to sleep." He brushed a strand of hair from her eyes. "God, you're pretty in the morning."

Ellie felt a warm blush creep up her cheeks. She knew quite well what she looked like in the morning and he was definitely too charming for his own good. But then, that's what she loved about Liam. He made her feel like the most beautiful woman in the world.

"Until I brush my hair and have my first latte, I'm a monster," Ellie teased.

"Then I better go out and get you coffee. I'll bring us something to eat, too."

"Maybe I'll take a shower."

Liam grabbed her waist and rolled on top of her, pinning her hands at her sides. Then he kissed her softly. "If you wait for me, I'll wash your back."

"Deal."

He kissed her again, then scrambled off the bed. "I'll be back in a few minutes. Don't go anywhere."

Ellie watched him leave, then moaned, turning her face into Liam's pillow. Last night had been so wonderful. She'd known it would be. How could it be anything else but mind-numbingly incredible with a man like Liam Quinn? He was so beautiful and sexy, and the things he'd done to her were just so...

She moaned again, then bolted upright, brushing her hair out of her eyes. She'd be waiting for Liam when he came back, but at least she had time to brush her teeth and comb her hair. She hopped out of bed and grabbed the Patriots jersey, tugging it over her head. Then she found her cosmetics bag and headed to the bathroom.

But instead of opening the second door on the left, Ellie opened the first and stepped into a room lit only by a red bulb on the far wall. She quickly turned around to leave, but then her curiosity got the best of her. Photos hung from wires stretched above tables and the single window in the room had been painted black. This was Liam's darkroom!

Her curiosity piqued, she walked inside. Photos plastered the walls and she stared up at the odd mix of images, hoping to find some piece of Liam in each. His portraits of everyday people were the most striking— waitresses, garbage men, traffic cops. She'd viewed photography in art galleries in New York and Liam's work was as good as any she'd seen there.

He was talented, and from the photos, she could see a tiny bit of his soul. He saw something through the lens that an ordinary observer would never see, a beauty in the simplicity of everyday life, an honesty that spoke more of him than his subjects.

She turned to examine the photos hanging from a wire above the table. They were strangely distant and a bit unfocused. Leaning closer, she tried to figure out what made the photos so special. And as she looked, a sick feeling twisted in her stomach. Ellie snatched a photo from the wire, then walked to the door and flipped the light switch.

"Oh, my God," she murmured. This was not a photo of an everyday Bostonian. This was a photo of her! In her robe! In her bedroom!

She hurried back to the table and began to pull each

photo off the wire. Each was of her, some of her in her apartment, some of her in front of her building, ranging in various states of dress and undress. For a long moment she couldn't take a normal breath. Her mind was numb and her heart had ground to a stop. Liam Quinn might be a very talented photographer, but he was also a sick, perverted, peeping Tom!

Ellie sucked in a long and ragged breath, that action serving to galvanize her. She raced around the darkroom, grabbing every photo and negative that even resembled her, determined to steal the last image from his possession. When she was finished, she headed for the bedroom.

She'd been so damn concerned about her safety that she'd never even recognized the true danger. In less than two minutes she'd dressed, packed her bag and snatched up the pile of photos and negatives from the end of the bed. Then the front door creaked and she heard footsteps in the living room. Ellie groaned softly. She'd wanted to leave without having to confront him. After all, a guy who took covert pictures of a woman might be downright dangerous. She'd tear up the photos, toss the scraps in his face and walk out, adding a threat to call the police if he ever came near her again. "That will do it."

But when she reached the living room, Liam wasn't there. His brother Sean was. He seemed surprised to see her, considering that he'd known she'd be spending the night. Ellie stalked up to him and waved the photos under his nose. "I want you to tell that sick, psycho brother of yours that I know what he's up to. If he doesn't want to end up locked away in jail or some mental hospital, he'd better stay away from me."

Sean opened his mouth, then snapped it shut again. "Okay," he said.

She stuffed the photos into her bag, yanked open the door, then made sure to slam it behind her. But when she reached the sidewalk, she wasn't quite sure what to do. She didn't have a car, there were no cabs or buses in sight, and she really wasn't sure exactly where she was.

"I should have never come to Boston," Ellie muttered as she hiked down the street. "I should have stayed in New York, kept my job there and put up with Ronald Pettibone. This whole move has been cursed from the start."

It hadn't been so difficult to get over the two break-ins, the near hit-and-run, or the brick incident with Liam Quinn around as a consolation prize. But now she had no choice but to add him to the list of disasters that had plagued her since she'd come to Boston.

"I can't believe I trusted him," Ellie murmured. She bit her lower lip to keep it from trembling. "I can't believe I slept with him." Her track record with men had gone from terrible to downright pathetic. She'd vowed to take time away from romance, to give herself a chance to recover. But Liam Quinn had been so sweet and so charming and incredibly heroic.

As Ellie walked she began to look at the events of the past few weeks in a different light. Yes, he'd come to her rescue so many times. But maybe he'd set it all up simply to get her into bed. "Oh, yuck," Ellie cried.

"He could be a sleazy creep as well as a sick psycho and a demented pervert."

She quickened her pace, following the sound of traffic toward a main street. When she finally saw an elderly couple strolling down the sidewalk, she hurried up to them. She explained where she wanted to go and they pointed her in the direction of a nearby thoroughfare, directing her to take the number nine bus to the Broadway T stop. Ellie assured them that she could find her way home once she got downtown.

But when she got on the bus, Ellie wasn't sure she wanted to go back to her apartment. Maybe she just ought to leave Boston—leave *everything*—behind and start over someplace new. She could go to Chicago or San Francisco. She could even go back to New York. She had friends there and the job prospects would be better. And she'd just slip back into her old life—minus Ronald Pettibone, minus *all* men. She had her purse and all her credit cards. She could replace everything in her apartment.

Ellie turned the notion over and over in her mind. It could work. And she'd certainly avoid seeing Liam Quinn again. She stared out the window of the bus at Monday morning traffic. Maybe it was time to find another place to start over.

LIAM KICKED OPEN the front door and stepped inside, Ellie's latte and his large coffee balanced in one hand, the paper bag of doughnuts clenched in his teeth. He yanked his keys from the lock, then closed the door behind him. As he walked into the living room, he was surprised to find Sean pacing back and forth in front of the sofa.

"Morning," Liam said, letting the bag drop onto a nearby table.

"Morning."

"I didn't realize you were here. I would have brought you coffee. When did you get in?"

"A few minutes ago," Sean said.

"Any news on Pettibone?" he murmured.

"None so far."

Liam headed toward his bedroom. "Well, I'd love to hang around, but I've got breakfast to deliver."

"She left," Sean called.

Liam stopped short, then slowly turned. "She left? What did you say to her?"

"Nothing. But she had a lot to say about you. From what I can figure, she wandered into your darkroom."

Liam groaned, then cursed. "I don't have to ask what she found in there."

"What did she find?"

"I developed the photos that I took from the attic window and they were...very...revealing."

"Naked?" Sean asked.

"No. What do you think, I'm some kind of pervert?"

"She does. And she thinks you're a psycho. A disgusting worm of a man."

Liam closed his eyes and groaned. "She said that?"

"No, but I'm sure that's what she was thinking. Jaysus, Liam, could you have screwed this up any worse?"

Liam aimed the bag of doughnuts at Sean's head and pitched it as hard as he could. But Sean's reflexes were too quick and he caught it. "Thanks. I'm starved."

"I've gotta go find her," Liam said. "I have to explain."

"You're not going to tell her the truth."

Liam shrugged. "I don't know what I'm going to say. But I've got to find some way to explain."

"You really like her, don't you?" Sean said.

Liam pulled his keys out of his pocket, then headed to the door. "That's a major understatement," he muttered.

He drove from Southie to Charlestown in record time, weaving in and out of traffic as he tried to decide what to say to Ellie. His first impulse was to come clean, to tell her everything and to hope that his instincts about her were right. But if they weren't, Liam knew she'd have no choice but to run. And then he'd never see her again.

With every other woman in his life, it had always been easy, a take-it-or-leave-it kind of affair. But Ellie was different. She made him feel confused and excited and frustrated and satisfied all at once. And when he thought about her walking out of his life, he got a sick feeling in the pit of his stomach.

Liam had been in love with a lot of women—at least he thought it had been love. But it didn't even come close to what he'd come to feel for Ellie in just a very short time. Was this real love, this crazy, wild, disturbing feeling that he had whenever he was with her?

They'd known each other less than two weeks. People didn't fall in love that fast, Quinn family curse or not. Memories of all his father's tales of the Mighty

Quinns drifted through his mind. Seamus Quinn had warned all of his sons about the dangers of succumbing to the powers of a woman. And for the first time in Liam's life, he understood what his father had been talking about. There was every chance in the world that this would end badly and that he'd end up with his heart in shreds.

He couldn't avoid the reality. Next month, Ellie Thorpe could be on trial for embezzlement. And the month after that, she could be in jail. Maybe that's what made it easy to fall for her. In the back of his mind, he knew it might end at any minute.

Liam parked the car in front of Ellie's building in Charlestown and hopped out. He took the front steps two at a time, then pushed the security buzzer, saying a silent prayer that she'd let him in. But the buzzer went unanswered. Either she was in her apartment avoiding him, or he'd beaten her across town. "Or she's already in the wind," he murmured. With a soft curse, he sat on the step, determined to wait.

He'd only been waiting two or three minutes when it began to rain—a cold, stinging, spring rain. Liam pushed up from the steps and jogged across the street. He'd wait for Ellie in the attic, and when she came home, he'd have all of his explanations in order.

As Liam unlocked the front door and climbed the stairs, he couldn't help but rewind the previous night in his head. He and Ellie had been so good together. It was as if her body had been made especially for him. Every curve, every sweet inch of flesh, was sheer perfection in his eyes. He could still feel her skin beneath his hands, her hair between his fingers, the warmth as he moved inside of her. And, even now, he craved it all again.

Liam pushed open the door to the attic and stepped inside. The room was as cold and musty as he remembered, the windows still grimy. Sean had left his video camera set up at the window and Liam strolled over and focused the camera on Ellie's apartment. He thought about the first time he'd stood in the window and watched her, wondering who and what she was. And now he felt as if they'd been destined to meet, as if some power greater than the both of them had conspired to put him in this attic and her in the apartment across the street.

He pulled the old chair up to the window and sat, determined to wait until she returned. But as an hour passed and then another, Liam started to worry. Maybe she'd run. She could have called Ronald and the two of them could have decided that it was time to go.

Liam fought back a surge of frustration. He knew in his gut she wasn't an embezzler, but his brain still managed to come up with enough doubt to make him wonder. He cursed softly, then fixed his gaze at the end of the street. The longer he waited, the more foolish he felt.

And then he caught sight of someone coming around the corner. He recognized her from the way she moved, the quick, determined stride. He took a deep breath, then slowly let it out. Though he'd spent the past two hours trying to figure out how to explain, suddenly Liam wasn't sure he could make it all sound right.

Hell, what did he have to lose? If she really was a criminal, then his explanation didn't matter. And if she wasn't, then he'd already screwed it all up so badly, it would likely never be fixed. She'd never trust him again.

He watched her start up the front steps to her building. And then she stopped. Slowly she turned around, her gaze rising up the building he now stood inside. Even from that distance, he could read her expression. She'd seen the photos and now she was wondering about his vantage point. Liam's breath seized in his throat and he waited.

His first impulse was to step back from the window, but instead he pulled the tattered curtain aside so she could see him, offering her a challenge and praying that she'd accept. She slowly crossed the street. When he heard footsteps on the stairs, Liam turned to face the door. It swung open a few seconds later and Ellie stepped inside.

She looked so beautiful—her hair wet, her color high—and so damn angry. Her eyes glittered with rage, her gaze suddenly fixed on the video camera at the window. She slowly crossed the room and pushed the curtains aside, the room flooding with light. Leaning forward, she looked through the viewfinder. "You must have a very nice little collection," she said. "Photos and video."

"It's not what you think, Ellie."

"Oh, no? You have no idea what I think."

"I can imagine," Liam said. "But it's not that bad."

"Oh, that's good," Ellie said, tears filling her eyes. "Because it looks really bad to me. It looks like you've been spying on me—and taking pictures—invading my privacy—like some kind of pervert!" She snatched up the video camera, tripod and all. "What kind of pictures were you taking? Should I expect them to end up on some Internet site? Or are they just for your private enjoyment?"

Liam's heart twisted. He'd never been good around emotional women. And once they started crying, he was completely at a loss for words. "Ellie, if you'd just—"

"I trusted you. I let you into my house. And into my body." With a soft curse, she heaved the camera and tripod out the window, the glass shattering and falling to the street below.

Liam winced. "That wasn't my camera," he said. "That was Sean's. But I guess that really doesn't make a difference, does it?"

"Why would you do this to me?" She held up her hand to stop his reply. "Don't bother answering. I don't want to know. From now on, just stay out of my life."

With that, she rushed toward the door, but Liam stepped into her path, blocking her way. "Just let me explain."

Tears tumbled down her cheeks. "I don't know why I thought you were different," she murmured. "But I never expected you to be...weird. This is all just very sick and you need help." She tried to pull away from him, but Liam wasn't about to let this be the end of it. "If you don't let go, I'll scream."

"Damn it, Ellie, let me explain."

"Go ahead. Tell me you're not some weirdo or some

pervert. Because, coming over here, I tried to make myself believe that you were."

"I was doing surveillance," he said. "I've been watching you."

She frowned, wiping her nose with the cuff of her jacket. "I don't understand."

"Sean is a private investigator and I was helping him with a case. He was hired by Intertel Bank in Manhattan."

"I—I worked for Intertel."

"I know. And right after you left, they discovered a quarter-million dollars of their money gone. Embezzled. And they think you did it. You and Ronald Pettibone."

"You think I embezzled money?"

"*They* do. The bank. And my brother." He inhaled a deep breath. "If you tell me you didn't do it, I'll believe you."

She stared at him for a long moment, doubt clouding her gaze. Then she shook her head. "I don't need to tell you anything. I don't owe you any explanation. Not after this." She yanked her arm from his grip and hurried out of the attic.

But Liam wasn't going to let her go. Not until he had an answer. He raced after her, taking the steps two at a time until he caught up with her on the second-floor landing. "Tell me the truth, Ellie. Did you and Ronald Pettibone steal that money?"

"Don't come near me again. If I see you on the street or in this attic, I'm going to call the police. And this time you'll stay in jail."

She hurried down the stairs and Liam cursed as he

heard the front door close. He fought the urge to go after her. Maybe it would be best to give her time. But he wasn't in the mood to wait for answers. She'd never said that she wasn't an embezzler. Had he really expected her to admit it? Hell, would it have made a difference if she had?

Liam sighed softly and started down the stairs. When he got to the street he searched the sidewalk for the video camera and found it resting against the building, one side smashed in, the tripod bent. A small price to pay for the trouble his brother had caused in Ellie Thorpe's life.

Liam shook his head. What about Ellie's deceit? She hadn't denied her involvement in the embezzlement. Not once had she offered an excuse. What price would she have to pay? Ten, fifteen years in prison? And how long would it take for Liam to forget her? Somehow he suspected it could be just that long.

"I should never have agreed to this in the first place," he murmured. "I should have told Sean to just take this job and shove it."

Though he'd already spent some of the retainer Sean had given him, the majority of the money was still in his bank account. If he gave it back to his brother, less the cost of a new video camera, maybe then his life could get back to normal. But first he'd start by spending the rest of the afternoon and evening doing what he did best—occupying a stool at Quinn's Pub.

He'd forget Ellie and everything that had happened between them—no matter how many pints of Guinness it took.

"SO, DO YOU LOVE HER?"

Liam sat at the end of the bar with Brian, the two of them sharing a late-afternoon meal. Quinn's Pub was busy for a weekday, filled with all the regular patrons, the after-work crowd and a few tourists, as well. The pub had appeared in the latest edition of Roamer's *Travel Guide to Boston* as one of the truly authentic Irish pubs and Seamus had been pleased with the boost in business—even if the regulars weren't.

This afternoon Dylan was behind the bar and Brian had stopped by for some dinner before he headed for the station. A half-eaten corned-beef sandwich sat on a plate in front of him. Liam had settled for a burger and fries.

"Aren't you going to answer my question?" Brian asked.

"Are you a reporter twenty-four hours a day?" Liam countered.

His brother grinned. "I'm used to getting the truth out of people and I don't think you're telling me the truth."

Liam reached out and picked up his glass of Guinness, then took a sip. "I don't know. I guess, until now, I really haven't thought about it."

"Either you do or you don't. It's that simple."

Liam paused. "It's never that simple. You know me. I need people to like me, especially women. I know what they want and I give it to them. And even after it's over, after I've moved on to the next woman, they still want to be friends."

"Sounds like you've been seeing a shrink," Brian teased.

Liam pointed to a dog-eared book on the bar. "Ellie left that at my apartment. She's always got one of these books open. Self-improvement." He held it up. *"Ten Steps to True Love.* I've been reading it. According to the book I'm 'Male Type No. 4: the Consummate Charmer.'" He flipped through the pages and read, "'The Consummate Charmer feels an almost pathological need for feminine approval. He'll say and do anything to complete the conquest, then will move on, finding another woman who will give him a fresh ego boost.'"

A frown furrowed Brian's brow. "That's not you."

"Oh, no? Sounds pretty sick, doesn't it?" Liam sighed. "I think it all goes back to our childhood. I've thought a lot about this and what happened to us when we were kids has made us into the guys we are today."

"Now you sound like a shrink," Brian said. "We're Quinns. We're not supposed to sink into self-examination."

"Maybe so. But look at us. Conor was responsible for holding the family together. And now he spends his life trying to protect the public the same way he protected us. And Dylan, he rescues the helpless. We were helpless when we were kids."

"And Brendan," Brian added. "He was always trying to escape. And now he can't stay in any one place for more than a month or two. He and Amy live like nomads."

"I haven't figured out you and Sean yet," Liam said. "But then I'm new to this."

"I suppose you're right," Brian said. "It's only natural that our upbringing affected who we are. Da gone for months at a time, Ma walking out when we were so young, Conor and Dylan and Brendan raising us. And then there were all those Mighty Quinn stories."

"But our older brothers got past that. Conor, Dylan and Brendan. They all fell in love. So it's possible."

"Maybe," Brian conceded.

Liam silently contemplated the notion of love while Brian finished his dinner. *Was* he in love with Ellie Thorpe? From the moment he'd first seen her through the lens of his camera, he'd been drawn to her. And then after they'd met, it had been almost impossible to put her out of his mind.

Time and time again he'd tried to rationalize his feelings. Why was she any different than all the other women who had walked in and out of his life? How had she managed to find a place in his heart when the others hadn't? His brothers might say that it was the Quinn family curse. That if he didn't want to love her then he shouldn't have saved her from the burglar.

But Liam knew better. Something had shifted inside him. Gone was his instinct to run, to avoid commitment at any cost. For the first time in his life he actually wanted a relationship to last longer than a few months.

"Maybe you should give it a chance," Brian said.

"You think?"

He nodded. "The way I see it, we've got one shot at it. And if we don't recognize it when it comes along, then we spend our lives looking. Look at Da. After all those years he's still in love with Ma. She walks out on him and he's thrilled to have her walk back in the door twenty-five years later."

"Not everyone has been happy to see her," Liam said.

"What is it with Sean?"

Liam shrugged, then nodded toward the door. "Why don't you ask him?"

They both watched as Sean strolled through the bar. He gave Dylan a wave and sat at the far end before noticing his brothers at the opposite end. He picked up his beer and started toward them. Liam fought the impulse to leave.

"What are you doing here?" Sean demanded, setting his beer down on the bar.

Liam groaned softly. He was in no mood. "Lay off, Sean."

"You're supposed to be watching Ellie Thorpe."

"I'm done. I don't need your money and I don't want the job. If you want her watched, then you do it yourself."

"Pettibone is still in town. We're this close. You can't quit."

"I can and I do. Besides, she knows we're watching her. If she embezzled that money, she's probably long gone by now."

Sean cursed softly. "She knows?"

"Yeah. After I left this morning, I went to her apartment and waited for her. I told her everything."

"Why?"

"She thought I was some kind of stalker so I had to set her straight."

Sean let out a tightly held breath. "She's gone."

"Maybe not," Liam said. "You're under the assumption that she's in on this with Ronald. I don't think she is."

"He's in love with her," Brian said, his mouth full of corned beef.

Sean glanced between the two of them. "Aw, hell. I should have know this was going to happen."

"I'm not in love with her," Liam said. "Not at all. I'm just not interested in doing your dirty work. If you want to watch her, then go ahead. If you want to chase Ronald Pettibone around Boston, feel free. I'm just saying that I'm done with it." Liam pushed away from the bar. "I'm going to play some pool. I'm sure there's some beautiful young thing who needs a partner."

He left his brothers to discuss the vagaries of love while he wandered to the back of the pub. Two girls in tight shirts and body-hugging jeans had commandeered the pool table, giggling and flirting with the men who had gathered to watch. Liam set a quarter on the corner of the table. "I'll play the winner," he said.

They both turned to him and graced him with dazzling smiles. He'd assumed that charming a new woman would take his mind off the previous woman. But as he watched them finish their game, Liam found himself comparing the pair to Ellie Thorpe—and they were suffering in the comparison.

He hadn't known Ellie for long—not nearly long enough to be sure that he loved her. But he knew the important things: she was honest and kind and stubborn and determined. She was passionate and naive and spontaneous and optimistic. And she had a natural beauty that didn't fade over time. In truth, Liam could go on and on, listing all the qualities about her that he admired.

He strolled over to the rack and picked out a cue. Maybe that was it. He didn't just need Ellie or want her, it wasn't just about attraction. He admired her. She'd walked away from her life in New York and come to Boston to start fresh. Though her history with men had been a series of disasters, she still believed in romance and passion. She wasn't jaded or cynical or bitter, she was just...Ellie.

"So, are you one of the famous Quinn brothers?"

Liam turned around, startled out of his silent contemplation of pool cues. "What?"

"Which Quinn are you?"

"Liam," he said. "Liam Quinn."

"I'm Danielle," she said.

"And who's your friend?" Liam asked, nodding toward the redhead.

"She's not my friend. And you don't need to know her name. She's going to lose this game." The blonde reached out and touched his arm, initiating a flirtation that Liam knew by heart. First, she'd touch him innocently. Then he was supposed to touch her. And then gradually the touching would become more regular and more intimate. And then, after a few hours, he'd kiss her, just a casual kiss at first and then— Liam groaned inwardly. Hell, it suddenly sounded so trite and silly. How many Saturday nights had he wasted charming women just like these two? And where had it gotten him?

Danielle sauntered up to the table and took a shot, banking the cue ball off the rail and sinking the nine in a side pocket. Then she wandered back to Liam, brushing against his body. "So are all the tales true?" she asked.

"Tales?"

"About the Quinn boys. Women do talk, you know."

"And what do they say about the Quinn boys?"

Danielle tossed her hair over her shoulder and sent him a sexy smile. "They say they're the best."

Liam groaned inwardly. He was just too tired to play the game tonight. Or maybe too bored. Or too preoccupied. But the best way to forget about one woman was to spend a little time with another. Liam grabbed the chalk from the edge of the table and ground it onto the end of the cue. "Well, we are pretty good pool players. As for the rest, most rumors are just that—rumors."

He watched as Danielle's friend knocked the eight ball into the wrong pocket. Then he grabbed his quarter from the end of the table and shoved it in the slot. The balls tumbled down and Liam reached for the rack.

One game of pool. And if he didn't find it... interesting, then he'd leave. Liam stepped back from the table and hung the rack on a hook on the wall. And if he managed to go fifteen minutes without thinking about Ellie, then he'd have to consider that a victory.

ELLIE STOOD OUTSIDE Quinn's Pub, staring at the neon beer signs that glowed from the windows. A damp breeze blew off the ocean, tingeing the air with the smell of the sea. She pulled her jacket more tightly around her body and took a deep breath.

She wasn't sure what she was doing here, but she knew she had to speak to Liam. She'd watched the attic across the street from her apartment and noticed no movement at the windows. Then she'd stopped at his apartment in Southie and he'd been out. Quinn's Pub was the next place to look.

Why was she really here? Was it for explanations? Or apologies? Or did she just need to reassure herself that things were completely over with Liam Quinn?

After their confrontation in the attic she'd been so hurt and angry that she hadn't had a chance to think. Her only impulse had been to lash out at him. But after she'd returned to her apartment and begun to clean up the mess, she realized that whatever Liam believed or did not believe didn't really make a difference. The management at Intertel Bank was under the impression that she'd stolen a quarter-million dollars.

Before she moved on to a new life, she'd have to clean up the mess from the old. And that meant proving her innocence...and finding a way to rationalize her very passionate but short relationship with Liam Quinn. Ellie looked both ways before crossing the street, then she jogged up the steps of the pub. Loud Irish music and the clamor of voices could be heard

from outside and she gathered her resolve, determined to remain unemotional when speaking with
Liam.

Satisfied that she was ready, she pulled open the
door and stepped inside. The first person she recognized was Liam's father, Seamus Quinn. Then she saw
Dylan, the firefighter, behind the bar with his father.
She caught his eye and gave him a little wave. He
looked at her for a long moment and then smiled and
motioned her over.

"Hey there, Ellie!"

She returned his smile. "Hi, Dylan," she said, raising her voice to be heard over the music.

"So you've decided to venture inside Quinn's. What
can I get you? Have you ever had a Guinness? Or
maybe you'd like something more suited to a lady's
tastes."

"Actually, I don't need anything to drink. I was just
looking for Liam. Do you know where he is?"

Dylan glanced over his shoulder. "He was down at
the end of the bar with Sean and Brian. But maybe he's
left. I'll just go—"

"No," Ellie said. "I'll go ask. Thanks."

She wandered toward the end of the bar and found
Brian and Sean. When they saw her, Sean turned to
look toward a small alcove in the back. A crowd was
gathered around the pool table and she saw Liam
there, standing next to a curvaceous blonde in skin-
tight jeans. The blonde leaned into him, wrapping her
arm around his, and Ellie felt a surge of jealousy
mixed with a healthy dose of anger. How quickly he'd
forgotten her.

She watched him for a long moment as he leaned over the table and made a shot. He had an athletic grace that made even the act of wielding a pool cue seem sexy and provocative. Ellie's gaze followed that of Liam's companion, her eyes fixing on his backside. Whether he and the blonde were together or not didn't change what she'd come to say.

She walked back to the table and waited for Liam to see her. After he took another shot, he glanced up, his gaze meeting hers. She felt the breath leave her lungs and had to force herself to take another. At first he registered surprise, and then he smiled. Without taking his eyes from hers, Liam tossed his pool cue on the table, knocking the balls in all directions, and circled around to stand in front of her.

"You're here," he murmured, his gaze scanning her features as if he hadn't seen her in years. "I thought maybe you'd left town."

She shook her head. "Can I talk to you?"

"Sure."

"Somewhere a bit more private?"

"Liam, aren't you going to finish our game?"

Liam glanced back at the girl he'd been with, her lips now pursed in a pretty pout. "I can't. Find yourself another Quinn brother. This place is crawling with them."

"I think I need to talk to Sean, too," Ellie said.

Liam called out to his brother and motioned him over. They all found a booth in a dark corner of the pub and sat, Sean and Liam on one side and Ellie across the table.

She tried to avoid looking at Liam, but it was hard.

He was staring at her, his eyes fixed on her face. Ellie forced a smile. "I don't know if you're still looking for Ronald Pettibone. I mean, you know where he is. But I think I know what he wants." She reached inside her purse and pulled out a music box.

"What is this?" Liam asked, reaching out to pick it up.

"Ronald gave this to me a few weeks before we broke up. And then right before I left New York, he asked if he could have it back. He said it was a family heirloom. But this isn't an antique. I was so angry at him, I refused. Then I left New York to start over in Boston. And the next thing I knew, Ronald shows up here. I think he may have been the one to break into my apartment."

"So do I," Liam said.

Ellie glanced over at Sean and he nodded in agreement. "And I think this is what he was looking for," she continued. "I had it in a box down in my landlord's storage locker. Ronald wouldn't have known to look there." She reached out to turn the music box over, her hand brushing against Liam's. For an instant she remembered what those hands had done to her, how they'd moved over her body, how they'd driven her wild with need. Ellie swallowed hard. "The bottom comes off. You just push that little clip forward."

Liam popped the bottom off, then glanced up at Ellie. "There's a key in here," he said.

Ellie nodded. "It's for a safe-deposit box and that bank is here in Boston. We came here on a long weekend and that's when he gave me the music box. We weren't together every minute and he may have had time to visit the bank. It's Rawson Bank. They have a branch a few blocks from the hotel where we stayed. I think that whatever is in that safe-deposit box has something to do with the embezzlement."

"If we could get in the box and—"

She shook her head. "Unless he put the box in my name, we won't be able to open it. I would have had to sign a card at the bank and I don't remember doing that, so I don't think that's the case."

Liam handed the key to Sean. "We'll check it out."

"No," Ellie said.

"No?" Sean asked.

"I have a plan. I'm going to call him and tell him that I know about the embezzlement and that I want part of the money in exchange for the key."

"Ellie, I don't want you to—"

She held up her hand, stopping Liam's protest. "I'm going to do this. I'll do it alone or you can be a part of it. But if I don't get it straight, then they're always going to think I'm an embezzler."

Liam slid out of the booth then reached over and grabbed Ellie's hand, dragging her after him. "Excuse us, I need to talk to Ellie alone."

As he pulled her toward the kitchen, Ellie tried to yank her hand away. "You can't talk me out of this."

When they reached the kitchen, Liam backed her up against a counter and braced his hands on either side of her, blocking her escape. He caught her gaze, his eyes intense and unyielding. "Ellie, this guy has already proved that he is willing to kill for this money. I don't want you taking this into your own hands. Sean and I will track down the money and we'll go to the authorities.''

"No," Ellie said.

"If this doesn't work, then Ronald is going to pass the blame to you. And he might walk away from this free and clear while you serve his time in jail. Do you want to risk that?''

"I didn't do this," Ellie said.

"I know you didn't.''

"Do you?''

Liam sighed. "Ellie, I never really believed that you were a part of this. Ask Sean. From the moment I met you, I questioned whether you could have done this. Do you think I would have gotten involved with you if I really thought you were a criminal?''

"And why did you get involved with me?''

"Because...I don't know...I couldn't help myself.''

"Or maybe you were just doing a job?''

"I know you're angry and you feel as if I deceived you and—''

"You did," she said.

"I'm sorry." He stared down into her eyes and Ellie willed the tears from falling. Slowly he brought his hands to her cheeks, cupping her face in his palms. He bent closer and she knew he was about to kiss her. At the last moment Ellie turned her head and stepped away from him.

"So how are we going to handle this?" she asked.

"I don't know what you want me to say.''

"I—I mean about Ronald. I think I should call him and invite him over. But I don't want to show him the key right then. He might...''

"Damn it, Ellie, you can't—"

"Stop," she said. She took a deep breath. "Maybe I can tell Ronald that I have the key in a safe place. Then we can go get it, then go to the bank, then when we're there, you can arrest him."

"I can't arrest him. Sean can't, either. According to Sean, once we have Ronald dead to rights, then we call the bank. They call the authorities, the grand jury indicts Ronald, an arrest warrant is issued and then they grab him. It's all pretty complicated."

Ellie looked up at him. "I can do this. I know I can get him to tell me what he did."

This time, Liam didn't hesitate. He grabbed her shoulders and pulled her to him, kissing her long and hard. She didn't pull away. Instead she smoothed her hands over his chest and wrapped her arms around his neck. When it was clear Liam wasn't going to stop until she did, she pulled back, and he pressed his forehead against hers. She wanted to tell him how he'd hurt her, how much she'd cared and how fragile she felt.

But Ellie wasn't ready to tell him what was in her heart. If he didn't return her feelings, then she was certain that her heart would break into a million pieces. And this time it wouldn't mend. She was in love with Liam Quinn, really and truly in love for the first time in her life.

"I should go," she said.

"No. We're going to talk about this. If you're going to do this, I have to know you'll be safe," he murmured.

"What should I do? Just tell me."

"You're going to call Ronald tonight and say you want to meet him. But it has to be somewhere that we can watch you. And listen."

Ellie nodded.

"Don't tell him what you want to talk about. Or if he asks, just mention that thing about finding a job. Keep it light. Make him believe that he's finally got an opening."

"I can't believe I ever cared about him," Ellie said. "I should have dumped him before he had a chance to dump me." She frowned. "The only thing I can't figure out is why he dumped me before he got the key back."

"He probably figured he could charm his way back into your life at any time. And he had to wait for the right time, once the suspicion was off him. But after you quit at Intertel and came to Boston, it must have taken him a while to track you down." Liam paused. "Maybe I should be there when you call him."

Though Ellie would have welcomed his support, she knew she couldn't fall back into their relationship so quickly. It was easy to love Liam Quinn, to depend upon him. But for once in her life she was going to take off her rose-colored glasses and see the guy for who he really was. A man who had deceived her, a man who had betrayed her.

"I'll call you," she said.

"I'll drive you home." He touched his finger to her lips before she could protest. "I just want to make sure you're safe."

Ellie nodded. She did feel much safer when he was with her—at least physically. But emotionally she knew that all it would take was another kiss and she'd risk losing her heart. Though he'd been there to save her from danger before, this time she'd have to save herself.

ELLIE SMOOTHED HER HANDS over the front of the black cocktail dress, then tugged at the neckline in an attempt to hide a bit more skin. She'd purchased the dress nearly three years ago for a special date she'd had with a Wall Street stockbroker, thinking that it might impress him. But then he'd called and canceled at the last minute and she'd never heard from him again.

When she'd pulled it from her closet, the tags still dangled from the dress. But at least it would be put to good use now. Tonight she was determined to trap a man and, in the process, to clear her own name.

She should be scared, or at least a little worried that she might not be able to pull this off. But since she'd met Liam, Ellie had learned that even she had the capacity to wield her feminine power. She may not be a femme fatale, but she'd gained a confidence that she'd never had before, secure in the knowledge that at least one devastatingly attractive and charming man found her sexy.

Ellie tugged on the hem, which rose to midthigh. But when she did that, the neckline plunged, revealing a fair amount of cleavage. "Just leave it alone," she murmured, adjusting her bra. She took a deep breath and examined herself critically. "I look...good." She turned to her side. "Really good. He's going to be putty in my hands."

"Is that what you're wearing?"

Ellie's heart skipped a beat at the deep sound of Liam's voice. He and Sean had arrived at her apartment several hours ago to plant a microphone. And since that time, Liam had been hovering over her, watching her get ready for her "date," silently observing—and driving her a bit crazy, as well. Sean had merely wished her luck and returned to the attic across the street.

She saw Liam's reflection in the mirror, his shoulder braced against the doorjamb of her bedroom. "What do you think?" Ellie asked. "I think it will do the trick, don't you?"

"Aren't you a little...exposed?" Liam snapped.

Ellie slowly turned to look at him. He was jealous. She smiled inwardly, taking a secret pleasure in that fact. "I want to entice Ronald, to show him that I'm not just some meek little wallflower. I need to appear confident and sexy, the kind of woman who would stand up for herself, who'd be willing to do anything to get what she wants."

"And you can't do that in a different dress?"

Ellie frowned. "What's wrong? You want this to work, don't you?"

Liam cursed, then turned on his heel and walked back to the living room. Ellie followed him. But as she caught up to him, she realized why he was so surly. "Are you upset because my dress is too sexy? Or because Ronald is going to see more of me than you think is proper?"

He turned on her, his jaw tight, his eyes icy. "You don't know what Ronald Pettibone is capable of. He tried to kill you more than once. I don't think it's wise to provoke him."

"But...but you're going to be here to protect me if anything goes wrong. And Sean is watching from across the street. I'm not afraid. I'm just worried that I might mess up."

"You know what we agreed on, right? If at anytime you feel unsafe, then you say the word 'hungry.' Ask Ronald if he's hungry. I'll be out of that bedroom in less than a second."

"All right. But what if he wants to go get the key right away?"

"Just tell him that the music box is in another safe-deposit box with your other valuables. And you can't get it until tomorrow morning. You'll get it and meet him at his bank tomorrow to pick up the money."

"And that's when we'll catch him in the act, right?"

"Right. Sean has talked to Intertel and they've called the authorities and told them that Ronald is here. They'll pick him up when he takes the money from the bank."

Ellie nodded. "And what about me?"

"You're going to have to tell your story," Liam said. "But I think it's pretty obvious that you didn't have anything to do with this. That Ronald was planning to use you as a scapegoat if things fell apart." He reached out and took her hand, giving it a squeeze. "You can do this, Ellie."

"I have to," she said, staring down at their inter-twined fingers. It felt so good to have him touch her again. Since he'd kissed her a few nights ago at the pub, they'd maintained an uneasy distance. Ellie still stung over the fact that he had deceived her. As for Liam, he seemed to want her to forget all his transgressions and pick up where they'd left off.

Ellie sucked in a deep breath and the knots in her stomach tightened. After this was all over she had vowed to make another fresh start, to find a new place to live, a new job, to put this all behind her. But when she thought about life without Liam, the pain moved from her stomach to her heart.

The buzzer sounded on the security panel and Ellie jumped. "That's Ronald," she said, glancing at her watch. "He's early."

"I'm going to be in the bedroom. I'll be able to hear everything he says."

"What if he wants to go in the bedroom? I mean, what if I have to—"

Liam's eyes narrowed. "If he wants that, then you just get him out of this apartment. Under no circumstance are you to—"

"No! I meant, what if he wants to see my apartment?"

He tipped his head back and sighed. "Just try to avoid that. If he does, then I'll hide in the closet."

She nodded, then reached over to the security panel and buzzed him in. Liam grabbed her hand and gave it a reassuring squeeze, then lifted it to his mouth and placed a kiss on her wrist. "Remember the word?"

"Hungry," Ellie repeated.

She waited until Liam was safely in the bedroom, then opened the front door, stepping out onto the landing. When she saw Ronald climbing the stairs, she pasted a smile on her face and tried to appear as nonchalant as possible. "Hello, Ronald," she said.

He gave her a smile, the same smile he'd given her hundreds of times before. But she'd never really noticed how smarmy it was. "Hello, beautiful."

"Come on in. Sit down."

He did as he was told, sauntering inside with a cocksure attitude. "Nice place," he said.

Ellie gritted her teeth. As if he'd never seen it before! "Thanks. Can I get you something to drink? I have a nice bottle of wine."

"Sure."

She escaped to the kitchen, giving herself a moment to breathe and to compose herself. So far so good. "Are you—" Ellie stopped herself. "Interested in something to eat? I have cheese and crackers." She'd almost said the secret word! "Focus," she murmured to herself.

"No," Ronald replied. "Just the wine."

When she returned to the living room, she found Ronald standing at her bookshelves, carefully examining the knickknacks she had on display. She held out the glass of wine.

"Thanks," he said. "I was just noticing. You don't have that music box that I gave you."

"Funny you should mention that," Ellie said.

"Why is that?"

Ellie sent him a shrewd look. "Sit down, Ronald. We need to talk." When he was settled on the sofa, Ellie took a tiny sip of her wine, marshaled all her resolve and jumped in. "About a week ago, I spoke with someone from the bank. Dana. Do you remember her?" She waved her hand. "It doesn't make any dif-

ference if you do or you don't. The point is, she told
me that you'd left your job. And she also told me that
someone had embezzled a quarter-million dollars
from the bank. Can you believe that?''

Ronald shook his head, an uneasy expression
crossing his face. ''That's terrible.''

''It is. What's even more terrible is that they have
two suspects.''

''How could that be terrible?''

''Because one of the suspects is me. And the other is
you. Now, I know I didn't do this, so that leads me to
only one conclusion—that you did.''

''Ellie, I can't believe that you'd believe that I—''

''Save it, Ronald. I found the key in the music box. I
know what you're trying to do. You broke into my
apartment a few weeks ago, looking for the music box.
You tried to run me down on the street and to kill me
with a falling brick, probably thinking that if you put
me in the hospital you'd have more time to search my
things. And when that didn't work, you broke in a second time and ransacked my apartment.''

''Really, Ellie, I don't know what you're talking
about.''

''I have the key,'' she said. ''It must be pretty important—important enough for you to search me out. So if
you want the key, then you and I are going to have to
make a deal.''

He stared at her for a long moment, obviously eval-
uating the situation and gauging her determination.
''Let's say I did embezzle that money. What do you expect to get out of this?''

''I could ask for half, since you've already made it

look like I was the one who did this. But I'm not a greedy person, Ronald. I'd be happy with fifty thousand. Enough to buy me a new start, maybe in San Francisco or Chicago."

"Do you have the key here?"

"No. It's in a safe place. If you agree to the deal, I'll get it and we'll meet at the bank and you can give me my share."

Ronald opened his mouth, as if he were about to refuse, then laughed sharply. "I think I underestimated you, Ellie."

"Most men do. They don't realize what they had until it's gone." She set her wineglass down, then stood. "So, do we have a deal?"

He rose and took a step closer. "I guess we do. And maybe we should seal the deal with a kiss? For old times' sake."

Ellie couldn't think of anything worse than kissing Ronald Pettibone, except maybe dental surgery without anesthesia. But she had a part to play and she didn't want to arouse his suspicions. She gave him a coy smile. "All right," she said. "To seal the deal."

8

LIAM CURSED SOFTLY, his mind conjuring up images to match what he was hearing through the crack in the door. He should have never allowed Ellie to do this, never put her in such a dangerous position. He wanted to pull the door open and to step into the hallway, curious to see exactly what type of kiss Ellie and Pettibone were sharing. But he knew he couldn't give away his position. Besides, Sean was watching from across the street. If he felt Ellie was in any danger, he'd been instructed to ring Liam's cell phone in warning.

Liam tapped his foot impatiently, waiting for them to start speaking again, wondering just how long the kiss would last. And then finally the sounds of their voices drifted down the hall to him.

"Now I know I underestimated you," Ronald said. "You've changed, Eleanor."

"Maybe I have," she replied in a teasing tone.

"You know, you and I could have a very comfortable life together."

"Oh, I don't know, Ronald. A quarter million doesn't go far these days."

"Oh, but I have so much more than that." He chuckled softly. "Haven't you wondered why it was so easy, why I got away with it?"

"Well, I have been curious."

There was a long pause in the conversation and Liam had to admit that now he was curious, as well.

"I've done it before. Three times at three different banks. I started small with a bank in Omaha, Nebraska. Then I changed my identity. That's the key, you know. Doing the job, then disappearing. After Omaha I hit banks in Seattle and in Dallas. With the investments I've made over the years, I've got two or three million in net worth right now."

"Ronald..." Ellie paused, "if that is your name, that's a pretty amazing story."

"You know what would be even more amazing? If you came with me. We could work together. It's a simple plan. I usually get an identity off the Internet. I find a banker who's looking for work and I assume his identity. The bank calls for references and I get the job. Then I set up a few dummy accounts and start moving money around. But here's the new wrinkle. I wait a month, maybe two, and I hire you."

"And why would you want me involved when you can just use any old girl at the bank for a scapegoat?"

"Oh, we'd still do that. I'd have to romance someone so I could shift the blame. I figure, between the two of us, we can increase our take."

"Just tell me one thing," Ellie murmured.

Liam knew she was touching him. Maybe she'd smoothed her hand over his chest. Or maybe her arm was draped around his neck. But the tone of her voice said it all, that deep, seductive tone she used when she was flirting.

"What would you like to know?"

"Tell me your real name, Ronald."

He laughed and now Liam could imagine Ronald touching her, slipping his hands around her waist, kissing the curve of her shoulder. Liam fought back the impulse to storm into the living room to place himself between them. This had gone way too far!

"When you tell me you're in, I'll tell you my real name."

"I'm going to have to think about this," Ellie finally said. "Can I give you my decision in a few days?"

"Or you could just give me your decision tonight. Much later tonight. After we've had a chance to get reacquainted."

This time Liam knew they were kissing. He heard Ronald growl softly and Ellie sigh. Anger bubbled up inside him and he wondered just how far Ellie was going to take this. She and Ronald had already agreed to meet the next day. Was she doing this just to torment Liam, knowing that he was listening to the whole thing?

"I think it would be best if we just took our time," Ellie said. "This is going to be a big change in my life. I'm going to have to give up a lot."

"We don't have a lot of time," Ronald said, Liam hearing the tension in his voice.

"The money's not going anywhere, Ronald. And aren't the best things worth waiting for? Just think of what you'll be getting. Money...and me." Liam heard the door open. "I'll call you, Ronald."

"Good night, Eleanor."

The door creaked as it closed and he heard her slide the dead bolt home. Liam waited a few more seconds then stalked out of the bedroom, nearly running into her as she rushed down the hall to the bathroom. He followed her through the door, not waiting for an invitation.

"Aack," she said, reaching for her toothbrush. "Aack, aack. God, I thought I was going to retch." She squeezed a healthy portion of toothpaste onto the brush and began to scrub her teeth and tongue.

"What the hell were you doing out there?"

"Did you hear what he said?" she asked, the toothbrush dangling from her mouth.

"Of course I did. I heard every word and every silence."

She continued brushing, her words garbled. "He's done this before. Three times. And Ronald Pettibone isn't even his real name. He wouldn't tell me what his real name was, but I'd bet we could figure it out from the banks he ripped off. He touched the wineglass. Maybe we could send his fingerprints in and get a match."

"Sure, I'll just run the glass down to One Hour Fingerprints and we'll see what they come up with."

She looked at his reflection in the mirror, then spit. "You don't have to be so sarcastic." Ellie grabbed a glass from the sink, filled it with water, then rinsed her mouth. "I bought us a few days at the most. Do you think Sean got it all on tape? He never even went near the flowers. That was the perfect place to hide the microphone." She grabbed a towel and wiped her mouth, then turned to him. "I did good, didn't I? Now Sean can give the evidence to the bank and they can have him arrested."

"You took too many chances," Liam said, his voice tight with anger.

"What are you talking about? I got him to admit that he'd pulled other jobs. I got him to admit that he took the money from Intertel—and from three other banks. And now he wants to run away with me so I can help him embezzle even more!"

Liam's cell phone rang and he pulled it out of his pocket and flipped it open. It was Sean.

"Let me talk to Ellie," Sean said.

Liam handed her the phone and watched as she listened to what Sean said. A wide smile curved her lips and she laughed not once but twice before she thanked Sean and said goodbye.

"He said I did a great job. And that he got everything on tape. And he said you should quit complaining and thank me."

With a low curse, Liam stalked out of the bathroom. He found the tiny microphone hidden in the flowers and extracted it, then looked directly across the street at the attic window. "Turn this damn thing off right now," he said. To assure himself that his request had been followed, he tugged the mike off the wire and tossed it on the table. Then he reached for the curtains and yanked them shut.

He turned to find Ellie watching him, her hands hitched on her hips. "What is your problem?"

"You're my problem," he muttered, crossing the room to grab his jacket from the sofa.

"I'm *your* problem? How? How am I your problem? The way I see it, I'm the one who should be angry. I didn't do anything. I didn't embezzle a quarter million dollars. I didn't lie about my motives in this relationship. I didn't spy on someone who shouldn't have been spied on in the first place. I'm the innocent one here."

"Right. You're innocent. I'm supposed to believe that after the way you behaved with Ronald Pettibone?"

"That was strictly professional," she countered.

"And what kind of profession were you engaged in?"

Her eyes narrowed at his thinly veiled insult and she walked up to him, her body just inches from his. "I should slap you for that."

"Go ahead," Liam challenged.

Her eyes blazed with anger and her breath came in short gasps, but she didn't rise to his bait. Her fingers clenched into fists and she started to turn away. In the blink of an eye, Liam's own anger shifted. He snaked his arm around her waist, pulling her against him and bringing his mouth down on hers in a hard, uncompromising kiss.

At first she fought him, but as his tongue invaded her mouth, he felt her soften in his arms, her body growing pliant beneath his touch. His hands slipped from the sweet curves of her hips to her backside, pulling her even closer, his need hot and hard between them.

A tiny groan slipped from her throat and she wrapped her arms around his neck, surrendering to his kiss. Liam knew if he picked her up and carried her to the bedroom, he'd meet no resistance. But he wanted Ellie to need him as much as he needed her, to

want him so badly, she couldn't survive without him.
So he pulled back, breaking the intimate contact and
leaving her to stand alone on wobbly knees. He turned
and pulled open the door.

"Wha— What are you doing?" she murmured, her
forehead wrinkled with confusion.

"Just showing you what you'd be missing if you decided to run off with Ronald Pettibone," Liam replied.
With that he stepped into the hallway and closed the
door behind him. He was nearly to the second-floor
landing, when he heard a crash of glass upstairs. And
then another.

"I guess I made my point," he said with a smile.

"ARE YOU READY?"

Ellie glanced over at Sean Quinn, sitting behind the
wheel of the car. He stared straight ahead, his gaze
fixed on the facade of Rawson Bank a half block away.
"I think so," she said. "I'm a little nervous."

"There's no need to be. Liam says that Pettibone is
already inside waiting for you. There are F.B.I. agents
inside, as well."

"The F.B.I. is here?"

"Ronald broke a few federal laws, too, so they're in
on the case."

"How will I know them?" Ellie asked.

"You don't need to know them. They know you.
You're wired for sound and if you get in any trouble,
just yell for help."

"Trouble?"

"Don't worry. It's a public place. Ronald isn't going
to pull anything."

Ellie nodded. "All right. Let's review. I go inside, I give Ronald the key, and I wait while he opens the safe-deposit box. When he comes back out, they'll arrest him. And then I can leave."

Sean nodded. "They took your statement for the grand jury, but you may have to give the Feds more information. And then there's Ronald's trial. Or trials, depending upon who decides to go after him."

"I'll have to testify?" Ellie asked.

"Probably."

"What if he gets off? Do you think he'll come after me?"

"He's not going to get off," Sean said. "If he's acquitted in New York, he still faces federal charges and he'll probably be extradited to Nebraska, Washington and Texas to stand trial for those other crimes. You'll be a grandmother before he sees the outside of a prison."

Ellie smiled. "Knowing my history with men, that could be a life sentence for Ronald."

Sean smiled, the first time she'd ever seen him smile. He was usually so intense, so preoccupied. But when he smiled, his whole face changed and he became the second most handsome man on the planet. Ellie had been grateful for his help over the past few days, through all the questioning and statements and explanations. Though Liam had been prickly and aloof, Sean had been steady and comforting, always there to calm her nerves. "I know he seems angry," Sean said, "but he's not."

"Liam?"

"None of this is his fault," Sean said, glancing over

at her. "I talked him into taking this job. I don't think he ever believed that you were a criminal."

"Did he ask you to say that?"

Sean shook his head. "Liam may be charming, but he's not that charming. I don't say things I don't mean."

"I believe that about you," Ellie said.

He took a deep breath. "Are you ready to go?"

"I'm ready," Ellie said.

"Then let's do it. I'll be a few yards behind you."

Ellie opened the car door and stepped out, then started toward the bank. As she walked, she replayed Sean's words in her head. She wanted nothing more than to believe in Liam, to trust in a future with him. But she'd been burned so many times by men far less charming than Liam Quinn. What if she did allow herself to forgive him? How long would it be before he betrayed her again? And if he betrayed her again, would she ever recover?

Yes, he was wonderful and sweet and sexy and handsome, all those qualities that a woman should want in a man. But these things made him attractive to every other woman on the planet. How long would it be before he found someone more exciting than Eleanor Thorpe, accountant and amateur private investigator?

Ellie knew she wasn't supermodel beautiful or accomplished in the bedroom. She wasn't particularly sophisticated or polished. She was just an ordinary girl who wanted an ordinary guy to love. The problem was, she'd stumbled on an extraordinary guy and she wasn't sure what to do with him.

A curse slipped from her lips. Now was not the time to review her romantic options! She had a job to do, one more task to complete before she could leave Boston and begin a new life somewhere else. Ellie crossed the street against the light and slowed her pace as she approached the front door of the bank. "I'm at the door," she said.

One of the security guards, standing inside, pulled the door open for her and she smiled at him as she passed. Was he one of the F.B.I. agents or just a guy doing his job? When she got inside the lobby, Ellie paused and looked around, wondering where Liam was standing. Then she saw him, sitting on a bench, reading a pamphlet. Their gazes met for an instant and Ellie's heart skipped a beat. Then she continued scanning the lobby.

Ronald was waiting at the far end, holding a leather briefcase and tapping his foot impatiently as she approached. "You're late," he said. "I thought maybe you weren't coming."

"I don't have a car," Ellie said. "I had to call a cab and it was late."

"Do you have the key?"

She reached inside her purse and handed it to him. His thin lips curled up into a smile and Ellie breathed a silent sigh of relief. Her part was done.

"So, Eleanor, have you thought about my offer?"

"I have," Ellie replied. "It's very tempting. But I think I'll wait and make my decision after we've completed this transaction. I have to know whether I can trust you."

"Why don't you come along and I'll show you the

rewards?'' Ronald took her hand and led her to a wide stairway. "The safe-deposit boxes are on the second floor."

Ellie couldn't refuse without arousing his suspicions. And what could he possibly do to her in a public place? There were so many people watching her that all she had to do was scream and they'd come running. "All right," she said. "We make the split upstairs then."

Ronald thought about it for a while. No doubt he had some plan to cheat her out of her share. And now he had to make a choice, keep her close or take the money and run. "Come to think of it, some banks have rules about who they let in the room while a box is open. Maybe you'd better wait outside."

"I still expect my share before we walk out of here," Ellie said. "I'll be waiting."

Ronald nodded, then started up the stairs. Ellie watched him until he disappeared through a doorway, reluctant to admit that she'd once been madly in love with him. "He's gone up," she said. She stood at the bottom of the stairs for a long time, waiting, wondering what to do next. She was afraid to move, afraid he might be watching her from above.

Slowly she turned to search the lobby for Liam, only to find him walking toward her, concern etched across his expression. "Come on," he said, taking her hand. "They just took him into custody upstairs. Let's get you out of here."

"No," Ellie countered. "I want to stay. I want him to know who did this."

A few seconds later Ronald reappeared at the top of

the stairs, flanked by two men in dark suits. His hands were cuffed behind his back and one of the men carried the briefcase. He glared at her as he descended and when he reached the bottom, he stopped.

"I knew I shouldn't have trusted you," he muttered.

"I guess you really did underestimate me, Ronald."

The agents grabbed his arms and began to drag him away. Ellie stared after him, a wave of satisfaction washing over her. It was over. She'd done what she'd had to do and now she was free to move on, to leave Boston and to make a new life somewhere else.

"Well, I guess that's it," Liam said.

"I guess so." Ellie turned to him, ignoring the ache that had settled inside her. She didn't want to say goodbye, but she made her decision. "Thank you—for everything you did. And thank Sean for me, as well."

"You can thank him yourself. I thought maybe we'd stop by the pub and celebrate."

Ellie knew if she went with him, she'd be drawn back in, hopelessly lost in her infatuation. Since she'd confronted him in the attic, she'd been faced with the reality that Liam had deceived her. He was no different than every other man in her life—in many ways he was far more dangerous—because he held her heart in his hands.

She'd thought about a future with Liam over and over during the past few weeks, but until now she hadn't been faced with a decision. All of her instincts told her to walk away. The other men in her life had hurt her, but Liam Quinn had the capacity to shatter her into a million pieces. Ellie took a deep breath, gathering her resolve. Now was the time to leave, if she was ever going to leave at all. "I should get home," she said, starting toward the door.

He followed after her, his long strides easily keeping up with hers. "Ellie, you've got to at least give me a chance here."

"Why?"

He grabbed her hand and laced his fingers through hers, pulling her to a stop. "I don't know." He paused. "Yes, I do. I need you, Ellie. You're the first thing I think about when I wake up in the morning and the last thing I think about before I go to sleep. And in between, I think about you a million times a day. I don't know why I can't get you out of my head, but it must mean something."

"It does now," Ellie said. "But believe me, it will fade. You're a man. Sooner or later you're going to feel compelled to move on."

"Don't lump me in with Ronald and all the others that have hurt you."

"Why should I believe that you're different?" Ellie asked, praying that he'd give her an answer she could believe.

"What if I loved you?" Liam asked.

Ellie sucked in a sharp breath and looked up into his eyes. She'd heard those words before and, in her experience, they usually signaled the end of a relationship rather than the beginning. Once a man said it, he believed that it gave him the license to stop trying. Then boredom would set in and then, one day, it would be over.

She'd never realized how jaded she'd become. Was she even capable of loving a man, capable of summoning the trust it required? She'd spent most of her adult life searching for the one person who would return that love. Just one person who'd make her feel as if she wasn't all alone in the world. "That's a nice sentiment, but saying it isn't going to change my mind."

"Damn it, Ellie, you can't just walk away."

"Yes, I can," she said, her heart aching with tightly controlled emotion. She reached out to touch him, then thought better of it. "Goodbye, Liam. Take care."

Ellie started toward the door, praying that, this time, he wouldn't follow her. Yet with every step she took, she was a heartbeat away from turning around and running back into his arms. But Ellie refused to go back. She'd made her decision and now she was prepared to live with it. She'd take control of her life again and think about what she wanted beyond a romantic relationship. When she'd come to Boston, she'd resolved to spend a year without a man in her life, to put all her bad experiences in the past and begin fresh. And now she had to follow through on that promise to herself.

But as she stepped out onto the street, Ellie fought back a surge of tears. Maybe she was walking away from the best man she'd ever met. Maybe she was making the biggest mistake in her life. But she wouldn't know for sure unless she actually walked away.

She took a deep breath and put one foot in front of the other. It was the hardest thing she'd ever done in her life.

LIAM SAT AT THE BAR, a pint of flat Guinness sitting in front of him. It was the lunch hour and there were only a few regulars at the bar. Seamus stood at the far end, chatting with one of them while Liam flipped through the latest edition of the Boston *Globe*.

He'd taken a nice photo of the governor opening a new factory in Woburn that should have made the paper, but it was nowhere to be found. Well, at least he'd gotten paid, whether they printed the photo or not. And he still had the money from Sean's embezzlement case burning a hole in his pocket.

He'd thought about buying a new lens or maybe a new camera. Or spending the money on some decent prints of his work, putting a portfolio together that he might be able to take to a few galleries in town. But the idea that seemed to stick in his mind was more of a gamble than a practical choice. He'd considered giving the money to Sean and asking him to find Ellie Thorpe.

She'd left Boston the day Ronald Pettibone was arrested. Liam had stopped at her apartment that night to try to convince her to stay, only to find her gone. Her landlord had told him that the movers would arrive the next week to put her belongings into storage until she settled somewhere and sent for them. He hadn't been able to tell Liam where Ellie had gone.

Since then, Liam had been at a loss to figure out where she was. He didn't know anything about her family or her friends. She'd mentioned San Francisco and maybe Chicago, but those were both big cities, and easy places to get lost in.

Liam had no choice but to accept that it was over. He'd never see her again. Unless he thought of a way to find her. It hadn't taken him long to realize the mistake he'd made, to admit how he really felt. He was in love with Ellie Thorpe.

"Hi, big brother."

Liam straightened as Keely strolled into the pub. He closed the paper and tossed it onto an empty stool. "Hi, little sister. What are you up to?"

"I'm looking for you," she said.

"Well, you found me."

She slid onto the stool beside him. Seamus wandered over and Keely asked for a club soda with a wedge of lime. Seamus winked at her and Keely gave him a warm smile as he served her drink. Though Seamus had only had a daughter for a year or so, he had quickly learned to enjoy the affection that Keely seemed to lavish on him. "And you'll have something to eat, too," he said.

"Corned beef on rye," Keely said, "with a slice of Swiss cheese. And fries."

Seamus wrote down the order, then tore it off the pad. "Coming right up."

"So, what did you want to talk to me about?" Liam asked.

"Photos," Keely replied.

"When and where?"

"No, this is about photos you've already taken. Remember those pictures of Boston landmarks that you did for Rafe's conference room?"

"Yeah."

"Well, Rafe was hosting a board meeting for some charity he works for and there was a woman there who is working on a coffee table book about Boston.

And she was very interested in talking to you about your photos. I think she might want to buy a few of them." Keely reached into her pocket and handed him a business card. "That's her number. She's expecting your call."

"Thanks. This is great."

"You know, I've always thought your photos were very special. I'm glad someone else agrees."

Liam reached out and slipped his arm around her shoulders, pulling her into a hug. "Does Rafe know what a lucky guy he is?"

"I keep reminding him," Keely joked. But then her smile slowly faded. "Sean told Conor about your friend Eleanor. And Conor told Olivia and Olivia told me. I'm sorry it didn't work out. Ellie seemed like a really nice girl."

"I guess the Quinn curse isn't much of a curse anymore. I followed the rules, I came riding to her rescue. She was supposed to fall in love with me and take me away from all this. But it didn't work. Instead, I fell in love with her."

Keely blinked in surprise, then laughed. "Wow. You're in love. That's a pretty important realization. Did you bother to tell her that?"

Liam nodded. "Yeah. In a roundabout way. I mean, I didn't come right out and say it. It was more of a what-if scenario."

Keely rolled her eyes. "What is it with you guys? Why is it so hard for you to express your feelings?"

"Do you really need to ask?" Liam nodded toward Seamus. "I guess you haven't heard enough of the Mighty Quinn stories to understand. Quinns are not supposed to fall in love. Women are evil and they are bent on destroying us in the end.''

"That is such a load of crap!" Keely said.

Liam shrugged. "The way I see it, I dodged a bullet. I'm the only Quinn who has managed to escape the powers of a woman."

"You're not free yet," Keely said. "After all, you're sitting here in the middle of the day, feeling sorry for yourself and trying to forget about the woman you're not in love with when I can clearly see that will never happen."

Liam laughed softly, then shook his head. "You do cut right to the heart of it, don't you?"

"I'm a Quinn. We don't sugarcoat things." Keely reached out and covered his hand with hers. "Go find her. Make this work, Li. Tell her how you feel and make it work. Don't let those silly legends and family curses take this away from you."

Liam groaned softly, then put his forehead down on the bar. "What the hell am I doing? I should go to her, find her and convince her to come back. But I'm scared that I'm going to be shut down again and then it's really going to be over. Right now, it's safer living in limbo, hoping that I still have a chance."

"You're just being a big wimp," Keely scolded. "Do you honestly think you're going to get what you want by sitting on your butt at this bar?"

He sat up. "But I don't know where she is," Liam said. He paused. "Not now. But I do know where she'll be. She has to testify at Ronald Pettibone's trial. And we're supposed to go to New York to talk to the prosecuting attorneys next month about our testimony. She's bound to be there."

"Then you have a month to figure out what you're going to say. A month to make it so good that she can't possibly resist."

"I'm not sure I can wait that long," Liam said.

"Don't you think she's worth the benefit of time? If you really care about her, then you need to be sure that you're acting out of love and not out of some need to soothe your bruised ego," Keely said.

Liam slid off his bar stool and grabbed his jacket. "Thanks, Keely."

He pulled his cell phone out of his pocket and dialed Sean's number as he walked to the door. But there was no answer on the other end. He knew Sean wasn't out of town and he wasn't working a case, so he was probably at home, catching up on his paperwork. Liam had done plenty of favors for his brother, now it was time for Sean to return one of those favors.

He just needed to know where she was, to make sure she was all right. Once he knew that, he could sleep again at night. For the first time in nearly a week Liam actually felt optimistic about his future. He had money in his bank account and a possible buyer for some of his photos. And he had met a woman he wanted to spend the rest of his life with.

Now he just had to find the right way to tell her.

9

THE Manhattan bookstore was a quiet respite from the congested traffic and throng of lunch-hour pedestrians outside. Ellie checked her watch, wondering if she ought to forgo browsing for a quick lunch. She had a half hour before she was due in the federal prosecutor's office to discuss her testimony in the embezzlement case involving Ronald Pettibone—or David Griswold. She'd learned from the prosecutor that Ronald was one of five aliases that her former lover had used.

The trial would take place next month and Ellie had been told that she would be called to testify. But today her mind wasn't occupied with thoughts of the trial, or even of her interview. Today there was every chance that she'd see Liam Quinn again.

A tremor of anticipation raced through her and she took a moment to calm herself. She'd been thinking about this day since she'd left Boston nearly a month before, wondering how it might feel to see him again, curious to know if their attraction had faded. She'd even taken the day off to get ready, spending most of the morning picking through her wardrobe and fixing her hair.

Ellie thought it would be simple to forget him. She'd been so hurt and confused and angry when she'd left him at the bank that day. Determined to make a new start, she'd decided to try a brand-new city. But on the way to her new life, she'd stopped by New York and Intertel Bank had offered her another job, as a reward for what she'd done to catch Ronald. Faced with the prospect of an exhausting job search in a new city, Ellie had accepted, gaining a promotion and a higher salary in the process.

It was as if she'd turned back the clock to a time before she'd met Liam Quinn, before she'd laid eyes on Ronald Pettibone. Her life had returned to normal—she had friends, a nice apartment in a familiar city. Only Ellie didn't really care for normal anymore. Normal was boring.

She glanced at the signs hanging from the ceiling of the store, directing customers to the different types of books. When she saw Self-Improvement, she fought the urge to check the shelves for something new. Since returning from Boston, Ellie had sworn off self-improvement. She was now learning to enjoy fiction. And she'd started collecting cookbooks.

It was high time to be happy with herself exactly the way she was. She didn't need to go looking for love. If it was meant to find her, it would. And all the relationships that had come before were part of her life's experience. "The right man is out there...somewhere," she murmured. "He just has to find me."

It sounded like a good plan but, in her heart, Ellie had a hard time convincing herself. Every time she pictured her future with one man, that man looked exactly like Liam Quinn, with his dark hair and his gold-green eyes. At first she'd tried a rational explanation—he'd simply been the last man in her life and his image still lingered in her mind. And then she'd decided that Liam Quinn had been the closest she'd come to her perfect man. But, finally, Ellie had been forced to admit that she was still in love with him.

She shook her head, unable to focus on the shelves of fiction in front of her. Her appointment was scheduled for eleven-thirty. There wasn't any reason she couldn't arrive early. Maybe Liam would be waiting, as well.

Ellie stepped out onto the street and wove through the mass of pedestrians, heading in the direction of Foley square. She wasn't even sure he was coming to New York today. Only a casual comment from the prosecuting attorney had given her a tiny bit of hope. Leslie Abbott had mentioned that she was going to try to interview all of them on the same day.

"I love him," she murmured, the thought repeating itself in her mind with every step she took. It hadn't been difficult to face the truth. Her feelings toward him seemed so natural and so right—even though he had deceived her and hurt her. But Ellie had gone through enough breakups to know that her feelings could be completely one-sided. For all she knew, Liam had moved on.

Ellie pulled open the lobby door and walked inside, ignoring the ache in her heart. Just the thought of Liam with someone else brought a flood of emotion. How could she have walked away? She'd allowed her anger to overwhelm her true feelings for Liam. She'd ruined something that could have been wonderful.

A security guard sat at a desk near the elevator. "Please sign in, miss."

Ellie grabbed the pen he offered and put it to paper. But before she signed her name, she scanned the list of people who had signed the book before her. Her heart skipped when she saw a name she recognized—Liam Quinn.

"Who are you here to see?" the guard asked.

"Liam Quinn," Ellie murmured, running her finger over his name. She glanced up, then realized her mistake. "I'm sorry. I'm here for Leslie Abbott."

"Seventh floor," the guard said.

The elevator took forever, grinding upward, floor by floor. Ellie imagined that Liam was on his way down while she was on her way up and they'd miss each other completely. Her mind whirled as she tried to come up with something to say when she saw him. "'Hello' would be a good start," she muttered. But after that?

The elevator doors opened and Ellie stepped into a tiny reception area. A receptionist greeted her and took her name, then invited her to take a seat.

"Ellie?"

She turned, then smiled, surprised to see Keely Quinn sitting near a potted plant. "Hi. What are you doing here?"

"I rode down on the train this morning with Sean and Liam. I have a cake decorating business here that I've been gradually moving up to Boston. But I still have a lot of corporate clients in Manhattan. I guess you're here for your interview."

Ellie nodded. "Is Sean in there now?"

"No, he finished earlier and headed back to the train station. Liam is in there now." She glanced at her watch. "They said he'd be done by noon. We were going to have lunch. Maybe you could join us?"

"I—I don't know. They might want to talk to me right away." Ellie took in a ragged breath. "So how is everything in Boston? How is...Rafe?"

"He's fine. But aren't you more interested in knowing how Liam is?" Keely asked, her eyebrow arching.

"I just...well, there isn't—" Ellie swallowed hard and forced a smile. "How is he?"

"He's been good," Keely said. "Busy. He sold some of his photos for a coffee table book on Boston and now he's going to have a show at a gallery. And he and Brendan have been talking about doing a book together. He also had a chance to show his photos to *National Geographic.* They didn't offer him a job, but they might in the future."

"It sounds like he's doing really well."

Keely nodded. "He isn't seeing anyone," she said. "Not since you."

"Hmm. Well, he won't be alone for long. He's a really great guy. There are plenty of women who will want him."

"Yes. But what he wants is what really matters," Keely said cryptically.

A long silence grew between them and Ellie fought the impulse to ask Keely what she was really trying to say. Did Liam ever talk about her? Had he been happy since she left? Did she think there was still a chance for them?

"And how have you been doing?" Keely finally asked.

Ellie took a deep breath. All this small talk was exhausting her! If she knew Keely better, she might be able to come right out and ask, Do I still have a chance with Liam? But she wasn't a teenager and she didn't need a go-between to solve the problems in her love life.

"I have a new job. And I just found a great new apartment. I'm doing really well. I've put everything that happened in Boston behind me. Actually, not quite everything—there's still this trial and…well, not everything."

Keely nodded slowly, then stood. "I'm going to see if I can find a cup of coffee. Would you like something?"

"No, thank you," Ellie replied.

She watched Keely leave, then folded her hands on her lap, trying to keep them from trembling. In truth, her stomach was so nervous she wasn't sure she could even take a sip of water. Everything came down to this, to the look on his face when he saw her, to the first words out of her mouth. Ellie groaned inwardly. So much for a brand-new start.

"Miss Thorpe? They're ready for you now. Down the hall and last door on your left."

Ellie quickly stood and hurried down the hall, her heart slamming in her chest. "Stay calm," she murmured. "Be cool."

She saw him as he stepped out of the conference room. He glanced up and their eyes met for an instant, then held. Ellie knew she was still moving toward him, yet she felt frozen in time. He looked so good, dressed in khakis and a sport jacket and tie.

"Hi, Ellie," he said, a crooked smile touching his lips.

"Hello, Liam."

The prosecuting attorney who stood behind Liam cleared her throat. "Miss Thorpe, if you'll just come inside."

But Ellie ignored her request. "How have you been?"

"I've been—"

"Mr. Quinn, I'm afraid you shouldn't be speaking to Miss Thorpe right now. Until we've interviewed her, she shouldn't be speaking to any of the other witnesses." Leslie Abbott crossed to Ellie and gently took her arm, pulling her toward the conference room. "If you'll just come with me, we can get started."

The door closed behind Ellie and her heart, pounding so fiercely just a moment before, now dropped. Was that all? Just a few words, a quick hello and nothing more? She'd plucked her eyebrows and shaved her legs just for this moment and it was over before it even began!

"Please sit down, Miss Thorpe."

Ellie took a place across the table from the court stenographer. Leslie Abbott sat next to her, setting her legal pad on the table in front of her. "So, let's get started. I understand that you and Liam Quinn were lovers," she said.

Ellie gasped. "What?"

"You heard me. Do you realize how this could affect our case? Look at this from the defense attorney's point of view. We have a private investigator who enlists the aid of his brother who in turn sleeps with the suspect's ex-lover—who was also a suspect in this case.''

''But I didn't know who Liam was when we...we became intimate. I just thought he was a regular guy. And then when he told me the truth, I was angry. After I learned that I was a suspect, I went to him and Sean and told them that I would help them catch Ronald—I mean, David.'' Ellie put her hands on the table and leaned forward. ''Is this going to cause a problem? Is Ronald going to get off?''

Leslie shook her head. ''I don't know. We'll just have to see how the case unfolds. But I have to warn you that Griswold will probably try to shift the blame to you. To make it seem as if you were the mastermind. We're in for a tough fight here, Miss Thorpe. Are you ready for this?''

''Do I have a choice?'' Ellie asked.

''I'm afraid you don't.''

Ellie closed her eyes, an image of Liam Quinn swimming in her head. Her words to Keely now seemed almost prophetic. She'd never be able to make a fresh start—with or without Liam—until she'd put this whole mess behind her.

And from the look on Leslie Abbott's face, that was going to take a lot longer than Ellie had anticipated.

''HERE'S TO Ronald Pettibone. Or David Griswold. Or whoever the guy was,'' Liam said, raising his pint of Guinness to Sean. ''May there be many more criminals like him for you to chase—and me, too, when I need a few extra bucks.''

Sean picked up his glass and knocked it against

Liam's. "Ten years, no trial. That's pretty good. Plus the bank got its money back and we got paid. Case closed."

"A few months ago I was wondering where I was going to get the money to pay the rent. And now things are definitely looking up," Liam said.

"What are you going to do with the money?" Sean asked, grabbing a handful of peanuts from the bowl in front of him.

"I don't know. Make some plans. I've got my eye on a new camera. And I thought I might do a little traveling, see if I can't get some nice photos to show *National Geographic.*"

"Any other plans?" Sean asked.

"What do you mean?"

His brother shrugged. "I don't know. I just thought..."

"Ellie?"

"Yeah," Sean said. "Ellie."

"Let me tell you, I was relieved when Pettibone took the plea bargain," Liam said, staring at the coaster beneath his glass. "I didn't want to see Ellie testify. After that interview I figured it might get pretty ugly. Ellie didn't deserve to have her personal life dragged out in public. It was a good trade. Pettibone gets to serve his sentence in a cushy country-club prison and Ellie gets to go on with her life. On the other hand I was disappointed I didn't get to see her. I had this whole speech laid out, how I was going to apologize first and then tell her how much she means to me."

"And now what?"

"I don't know," Liam said. "I guess I have to figure

out another way to get her back. It's gotta be something really great—so she can't possibly say no."

"And while you're thinking something up, she's probably getting on with her life," Sean said.

"What is that supposed to mean?"

"Hell, if you don't know, I'm not going to tell you." Sean took another sip of his beer, then slid off his bar stool. "I've got to go. Tell Da I can tend bar tomorrow night."

"And you and I are going to look for a wedding present for Brendan and Amy tomorrow, right? And we have to go get fitted for our tuxes, too."

Sean nodded and waved as he strode out of the bar. Seamus wandered down to the end and picked up Liam's nearly empty glass. "Another?" he asked.

Liam shook his head. "Nah. I better get going. Sean said he'll work tomorrow night. And I think I'm good for the weekend."

"Ah, you're a pitiful sight, boyo," Seamus commented, wiping the bar with a damp rag. "Ya sit here every night moonin' over that girl and where does it get ya?"

"Da, I don't need advice on my love life from you. We all know where you stand on the subject of women. Except, of course, for Ma."

"I'm just sayin' that ya got to stand up and be a man. Get busy livin' or get busy lovin'. This in-between makes ya look like a bleedin' gombeen."

Liam grabbed his jacket. "Are you going to tell me one of those Mighty Quinn stories now?"

"Maybe you could use one," he said.

Shaking his head, Liam started toward the door,

then heard Seamus softly call his name. He glanced over and saw his father nod his head toward the other end of the bar. Ellie stood next to a bar stool near the door, her hands clutched in front of her. Liam stopped dead in his tracks and his breath froze in his throat. He'd seen her just once in the past month, those few precious seconds outside the conference room in New York. But in the days that had followed, he'd imagined this moment over and over again, dreamed about it at night, carefully considered what he might say.

He slowly approached her, his gaze fixed on hers. God, she looked pretty. She wore a cotton dress with a little sweater. Her dark hair fell in waves over her shoulders. "You're here," he said.

Ellie nodded. "I wasn't sure if I should come."

"No," Liam said. "I'm glad you came. It...it's good to see you, Ellie."

She stared down at her fingertips, painted a pretty shade of pink. "I'm just in town for the day and I had a few things to say. I thought I'd get a chance to see you at the trial."

"Yeah, the trial. I guess I'm kind of glad we didn't have to go through that."

"That's what I came to tell you." She risked a glance up at him. "I want you to know that there are no hard feelings. I understand now that you were just doing a job and that your only concern was putting Ronald Pettibone in jail—where he belonged."

"That wasn't my only concern, Ellie." He reached out to touch her arm. "And it wasn't just a job. I was with you because I wanted to be with you, not because I had to be."

A blush stained her cheeks. "You don't have to say that. I'm really all right with everything that happened."

"Well, I'm not," Liam countered. "Ellie, I haven't been able to stop thinking about you."

She stared at him for a long moment and Liam was sure she was about to turn and run. But then she swallowed hard and attempted to smile. "And I haven't stopped thinking about you, either," Ellie said. "I made a mistake and—"

"No, I'm the one who made the mistake." Liam couldn't contain his excitement. She still cared! "I never should have let you go."

"I never should have gone."

Liam glanced around the pub, then grabbed Ellie's hand and pulled her toward the door. They stepped outside into the late-afternoon sun. A warm breeze blew from the south and summer was in the air. He pulled Ellie along the sidewalk until he was sure they were completely alone. "What does this mean?"

"I don't know," she said, her voice trembling. "I just feel like we left things unfinished."

"Me, too," Liam said. "Like there's more to us than what we had. That if we just had a little more time, we would realize how great it really was."

"So what *does* this mean?" Ellie asked.

Liam's gaze skimmed over her pretty face. "It means that I want to be with you, Ellie. I want to see where this could go." He reached up and cupped her face in his palms, then kissed her, lingering over her lips for a long time. "I love you. I don't think I really knew that for sure until this very moment. But I can't even think of a future without you in it."

"That's a good thing," Ellie said, her mouth curving into a warm smile. "Because I just accepted a new job at the Boston branch of Intertel. I thought I might come here and get a new start." She reached up and brushed his hair back from his eyes. "And just so you know, I love you, too."

Liam tipped his head back and laughed. Then he grabbed her again and pulled her into his embrace, this time kissing her like a man in love. He'd spent so long avoiding a real relationship and now he understood why—he'd been waiting for Ellie Thorpe to come into his life.

"You know, I'm going to ask you to marry me," Liam said. "And we're going to have a family and we're going to live happily ever after. Are you all right with that?"

"You're not proposing to me now, are you?" Ellie asked, looking slightly alarmed.

"No. I'm just warning you that I will. And it will be great. And you won't be able to say no."

"You're pretty confident, aren't you?"

"Yeah, I am. I've been doing a little reading. *Ten Steps to True Love.* Have you read it?"

Ellie blushed, then wriggled in his arms. "I think I have. But you know, I've decided to give up the self-help books. Instead I'm just going to listen to my heart."

"And what does your heart say?"

"That I'm glad you came to my rescue that night. And that I'm glad I decided to come to Boston today."

Liam chuckled, thinking back to all the tales of the Mighty Quinns he'd been told as a child, to the Quinn "curse" that had befallen his three oldest brothers. He smoothed his hands over Ellie's shoulders and kissed her forehead. Now he knew why Conor and Dylan and Brendan had laughed when their father brought up the curse. It wasn't a curse at all. It was a gift.

And Liam was going to spend the rest of his life thankful for the gift, for the fateful events that brought Ellie Thorpe into his life...and for the love that would keep her there.

_____ **Epilogue** _____

"ARE YOU READY YET?"

Ellie stared at her reflection in the mirror, then touched her fingers to the string of pearls that circled her throat. Liam had given them to her as an anniversary gift, in honor of one month together. She smiled. One month and so much had changed. They'd settled into a life together. Liam's career had begun to flourish and Ellie had a brand-new job at Intertel Boston. They'd begun a search for the perfect apartment, living at Liam's place while they looked. And she'd fallen more deeply in love with the man of her dreams.

"Perfect," she murmured, pleased with how the necklace looked with her gown.

Liam knocked impatiently on the bathroom door. "We're going to be late, Ellie."

"I'm coming," she said. "Just give me a few more minutes."

"Amy told me that I have to be there at exactly six p.m."

"It's five-thirty," Ellie called. "The wedding doesn't start until seven. We have plenty of time. The church is only fifteen minutes away."

Ellie smoothed her hands over her gown. The pale blue silk had a strapless bodice that fit her perfectly. The beading gave it an elegant look and the narrow waist flared into a full skirt that rustled when she walked.

"Are you dressed?" Ellie asked, picking up her earrings.

"All but the tie. I can't get it straight. And these studs are too small to work. Why don't they just put buttons on the shirt?"

"Because studs are so sexy." She grabbed her lipstick and touched up, then dropped it in her purse. "All right, I'm ready."

Ellie pulled the bathroom door open and walked out. Liam stood at the end of the hallway, his tux jacket on, his pleated shirt unbuttoned to the waist and his bow tie draped around his neck.

He was fussing with his cuff links, then glanced up at her. His jaw dropped and he stared. "Wow!"

Ellie smiled, warmed by his compliment. Even though they'd been living together for a month, Liam still found a way to charm her every single day, to make her feel like the most beautiful woman in the world. "Thank you."

"You look—wow."

"You look pretty nice yourself. Do you think they'd let you keep that tux for a few days? You could wear it around the apartment."

"I look like a waiter," Liam said, tugging on the front of his jacket. Then he grinned. "But I feel like James Bond."

"You're much more handsome than James," Ellie teased. She took the studs from his palm and began to work at the front of his shirt. Her fingers brushed against his naked chest and Ellie felt a tiny tremor run through her. They'd made love countless times since she returned to Boston, yet a simple touch was enough to pique her desire. Would she ever have enough of him? Ellie couldn't imagine a time when she wouldn't crave his touch or the taste of his mouth or the feel of his hands on her body.

"There," she said, smoothing her hand down the front of his shirt. "That looks nice."

"So you think studs are sexy, huh?" Liam asked. "Why is that?"

"Well, a girl can just yank open the shirt and the studs go flying," Ellie explained. "I saw it in a movie once. Very provocative."

"You mean, like this?" Liam grabbed the front of his shirt and tugged, and just as Ellie had described, the studs went flying, skittering across the hardwood floor of the bedroom.

"What are you doing?" she cried, trying to restore order to his shirt.

Liam grabbed her around the waist and pulled her toward the bed. "You said we had time. We don't have to be to the church for a half hour."

"Twenty-five minutes," she corrected, pushing against his chest.

"An hour and twenty-five minutes," Liam countered.

"If we're late, Brendan will have your head. And Amy won't speak to me."

"They're in love. They'll understand." Liam reached around for the zipper of her dress, then slowly slid it down. When he reached the small of her back, he stepped back, then brushed the dress from her shoulders. It fell to the floor in a heap around her feet. Ellie groaned in protest, but stepped out of it.

"I thought the dress was nice," he murmured, his gaze raking her body, "but that underwear should be outlawed."

Ellie giggled, then turned him around. She helped him out of his jacket and carefully folded it on a nearby chair. "Fifteen minutes," she said. "Then we have to go." She slipped his suspenders over his shoulders and tugged his shirt out of his trousers. They undressed each other, playing at a mutual strip-tease, anticipating what they were about to share. And when they'd removed the last item of clothing, Liam growled playfully and dragged her down on the bed.

"You're beautiful in that dress," he murmured, kissing her neck. "But you're even more beautiful out of it."

"We shouldn't be doing this," Ellie said.

He rolled on top of her, nestling into her hips, his desire hot against her belly. Then he reached down and fingered her pearls. "They look nice," he said. "Better without the dress. But don't you think they're a little plain?"

"No!" Ellie said, running the pearls between her fingers. "I think they're beautiful."

"There're probably a lot of different things that you would have liked better—a new sofa, a blender, maybe a new vacuum cleaner."

"Never. I love these pearls. They're all I could ever want."

Liam shoved his hand under the pillow and pulled

out a small velvet box. "Then I probably shouldn't give you this."

Ellie stared at the box for a long time, stunned by the sudden turn of events. She reached out to take the box from his palm, but before she could, he closed his hand. "I should really do this properly," Liam said. He rolled off the bed, and knelt beside it, completely naked. He braced his arms on the mattress and set the box in front of him.

Ellie lay on her stomach, facing him. Her gaze took in his handsome face, his rumpled hair and his gorgeous eyes. "What are you doing?"

"I'm going to ask you to marry me, Ellie. I was going to save this for later, but when we walk into that church today, I want you to know that it's going to be our turn soon. I know it's fast, but I love you, and that's never going to change." He opened up the box and removed the ring. "Will you, Ellie? Will you marry me?"

He took her hand and held the ring at the end of her finger, waiting for her answer. She stared at the diamond and it twinkled back at her, as if urging her to say yes.

She'd known they were headed in this direction, but after all that had happened in her past, she wouldn't let herself believe that it really could happen, that she'd find a man who wanted to spend his life with her.

And now she had and he was the most wonderful man in the world, the answer to all her dreams and the hero who'd stolen her heart. Ellie bit her bottom lip, a tear trickling down her cheek. "I will marry you, Liam," she murmured.

He slipped the ring on her finger, then jumped up on the bed, pulling her into his embrace and giving her a long and very passionate kiss. "I guess the Quinn curse is still alive and well," Liam said, nuzzling her neck.

"The Quinn curse?"

"It's a long story," he said. "And we have years for you to hear all the Mighty Quinn tales. I'll tell them all to you, I promise. But right now, all I really want to do is kiss you."

Ellie wrapped her arms around his neck and touched her lips to his. And as she lost herself in the taste of him, in the warmth of his body lying across hers, and in the sound of his voice, Ellie knew that there was nothing more that she needed in life. She had her hero. She had her white knight.

She had her Mighty Quinn.

AMERICAN HEROES

These men are heroes—
strong, fearless...
And impossible to resist!

**Join bestselling authors Lori Foster, Donna Kauffman
and Jill Shalvis as they deliver up**

MEN OF COURAGE

**Harlequin anthology
May 2003**

Followed by *American Heroes* miniseries
in Harlequin Temptation

**RILEY by Lori Foster
June 2003**

**SEAN by Donna Kauffman
July 2003**

**LUKE by Jill Shalvis
August 2003**

Don't miss this sexy new miniseries by some of
Temptation's hottest authors!

Available at your favorite retail outlet.

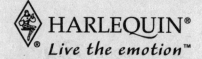

HARLEQUIN®
Live the emotion™

Visit us at www.eHarlequin.com

HTAH

Is your man too good to be true?

Hot, gorgeous AND romantic?
If so, he could be a Harlequin® Blaze™ series cover model!

Our grand-prize winners will receive a trip for two to New York City to shoot the cover of a Blaze novel, and will stay at the luxurious Plaza Hotel. Plus, they'll receive $500 U.S. spending money! The runner-up winners will receive $200 U.S. to spend on a romantic dinner for two.

It's easy to enter!

In 100 words or less, tell us what makes your boyfriend or spouse a true romantic and the perfect candidate for the cover of a Blaze novel, and include in your submission two photos of this potential cover model.

All entries must include the written submission of the contest entrant, two photographs of the model candidate and the Official Entry Form and Publicity Release forms completed in full and signed by both the model candidate and the contest entrant. Harlequin, along with the experts at Elite Model Management, will select a winner.

For photo and complete Contest details, please refer to the Official Rules on the next page. All entries will become the property of Harlequin Enterprises Ltd. and are not returnable.

Please visit www.blazecovermodel.com to download a copy of the Official Entry Form and Publicity Release Form or send a request to one of the addresses below.

Please mail your entry to: **Harlequin Blaze Cover Model Search**

In U.S.A.	In Canada
P.O. Box 9069	P.O. Box 637
Buffalo, NY	Fort Erie, ON
14269-9069	L2A 5X3

No purchase necessary. Contest open to Canadian and U.S. residents who are 18 and over. Void where prohibited. Contest closes September 30, 2003.

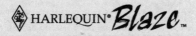

HBCVRMODEL1

HARLEQUIN BLAZE COVER MODEL SEARCH CONTEST 3569 OFFICIAL RULES
NO PURCHASE NECESSARY TO ENTER

1. To enter, submit two (2) 4" x 6" photographs of a boyfriend or spouse (who must be 18 years of age or older) taken no later than three (3) months from the time of entry: a close-up, waist up, shirtless photograph; and a fully clothed, full-length photograph, then, tell us, in 100 words or fewer, why he should be a Harlequin Blaze cover model and how he is romantic. Your complete "entry" must include: (i) your essay, (ii) the Official Entry Form and Publicity Release Form printed below completed and signed by you (as "Entrant"), (iii) the photographs (with your hand-written name, address and phone number, and your model's name, address and phone number on the back of each photograph), and (iv) the Publicity Release Form and Photograph Representation Form printed below completed and signed by your model (as "Model"), and should be sent via first-class mail to either: Harlequin Blaze Cover Model Search Contest 3569, P.O. Box 9069, Buffalo, NY, 14269-9069, or Harlequin Blaze Cover Model Search Contest 3569, P.O. Box 637, Fort Erie, Ontario L2A 5X3. All submissions must be in English and be received no later than September 30, 2003. Limit: one entry per person, household or organization. **Purchase or acceptance of a product offer does not improve your chances of winning.** All entry requirements must be strictly adhered to for eligibility and to ensure fairness among entries.

2. Ten (10) Finalist submissions (photographs and essays) will be selected by a panel of judges consisting of members of the Harlequin editorial, marketing and public relations staff, as well as a representative from Elite Model Management (Toronto) Inc., based on the following criteria:

Aptness/Appropriateness of submitted photographs for a Harlequin Blaze cover—70%
Originality of Essay—20%
Sincerity of Essay—10%

In the event of a tie, duplicate finalists will be selected. The photographs submitted by finalists will be posted on the Harlequin website no later than November 15, 2003 (at www.blazecovermodel.com), and viewers may vote, in rank order, on their favorite(s) to assist in the panel of judges' final determination of the Grand Prize and Runner-up winning entries based on the above judging criteria. All decisions of the judges are final.

3. All entries become the property of Harlequin Enterprises Ltd. and none will be returned. Any entry may be used for future promotional purposes. Elite Model Management (Toronto) Inc. and/or its partners, subsidiaries and affiliates operating as "Elite Model Management" will have access to all entries including all personal information, and may contact any Entrant and/or Model in its sole discretion for their own business purposes. Harlequin and Elite Model Management (Toronto) Inc. are separate entities with no legal association or partnership whatsoever having no power to bind or obligate the other or create any expressed or implied obligation or responsibility on behalf of the other, such that Harlequin shall not be responsible in any way for any acts or omissions of Elite Model Management (Toronto) Inc. or its partners, subsidiaries and affiliates in connection with the Contest or otherwise and Elite Model Management shall not be responsible in any way for any acts or omissions of Harlequin or its partners, subsidiaries and affiliates in connection with the contest or otherwise.

4. All Entrants and Models must be residents of the U.S. and Canada, be 18 years of age or older, and have no prior criminal convictions. The contest is not open to any Model that is a professional model and/or actor in any capacity at the time of the entry. Contest void wherever prohibited by law; all applicable laws and regulations apply. Any litigation within the Province of Quebec regarding the conduct or organization of a publicity contest may be submitted to the Régie des alcools, des courses et des jeux for a ruling, and any litigation regarding the awarding of a prize may be submitted to the Régie only for the purpose of helping the parties reach a settlement. Employees and immediate family members of Harlequin Enterprises Ltd., D.L. Blair, Inc., Elite Model Management (Toronto) Inc. and their parents, affiliates, subsidiaries and all other agencies, entities and persons connected with the use, marketing or conduct of this Contest are not eligible to enter. Acceptance of any prize offered constitutes permission to use Entrants' and Models' names, essay submissions, photographs or other likenesses for the purposes of advertising, trade, publication and promotion on behalf of Harlequin Enterprises Ltd., its parent, affiliates, subsidiaries, assigns and other authorized entities involved in the judging and promotion of the contest without further compensation to any Entrant or Model, unless prohibited by law.

5. Finalists will be determined no later than October 30, 2003. Prize Winners will be determined no later than January 31, 2004. Grand Prize Winners (consisting of winning Entrant and Model) will be required to sign and return Affidavit of Eligibility/Release of Liability and Model Release forms within thirty (30) days of notification. Non-compliance with this requirement and within the specified time period will result in disqualification and an alternate will be selected. Any prize notification returned as undeliverable will result in the awarding of the prize to an alternate set of winners. All travelers (or parent/legal guardian of a minor) must execute the Affidavit of Eligibility/Release of Liability prior to ticketing and must possess required travel documents (e.g. valid photo ID) where applicable. Travel dates specified by Sponsor but no later than May 30, 2004.

6. Prizes: One (1) Grand Prize—the opportunity for the Model to appear on the cover of a paperback book from the Harlequin Blaze series, and a 3 day/2 night trip for two (Entrant and Model) to New York, NY for the photo shoot of Model which includes round-trip coach air transportation from the commercial airport nearest the winning Entrant's home to New York, NY, (or, in lieu of air transportation, $100 cash payable to Entrant and Model, if the winning Entrant's home is within 250 miles of New York, NY), hotel accommodations (double occupancy) at the Plaza Hotel and $500 cash spending money payable to Entrant and Model, (approximate prize value: $8,000), and one (1) Runner-up Prize of $200 cash payable to Entrant and Model for a romantic dinner for two (approximate prize value: $200). Prizes are valued in U.S. currency. Prizes consist of only those items listed as part of the prize. No substitution of prize(s) permitted by winners. All prizes are awarded jointly to the Entrant and Model of the winning entries, and are not severable - prizes and obligations may not be assigned or transferred. Any change to the Entrant and/or Model of the winning entries will result in disqualification and an alternate will be selected. Taxes on prize are the sole responsibility of winners. Any and all expenses and/or items not specifically described as part of the prize are the sole responsibility of winners. Harlequin Enterprises Ltd. and D.L. Blair, Inc., their parents, affiliates, and subsidiaries are not responsible for errors in printing of Contest entries and/or game pieces. No responsibility is assumed for lost, stolen, late, illegible, incomplete, inaccurate, non-delivered, postage due or misdirected mail or entries. In the event of printing or other errors which may result in unintended prize values or duplication of prizes, all affected game pieces or entries shall be null and void.

7. Winners will be notified by mail. For winners' list (available after March 31, 2004), send a self-addressed, stamped envelope to: Harlequin Blaze Cover Model Search Contest 3569 Winners, P.O. Box 4200, Blair, NE 68009-4200, or refer to the Harlequin website (at www.blazecovermodel.com).

Contest sponsored by Harlequin Enterprises Ltd., P.O. Box 9042, Buffalo, NY 14269-9042.

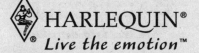